To Paul and Merrill,

   May you have many new Train Stops of adventures with suprise endings. Enjoy.

          Yours, yes,

          Larry Frank

train
stops

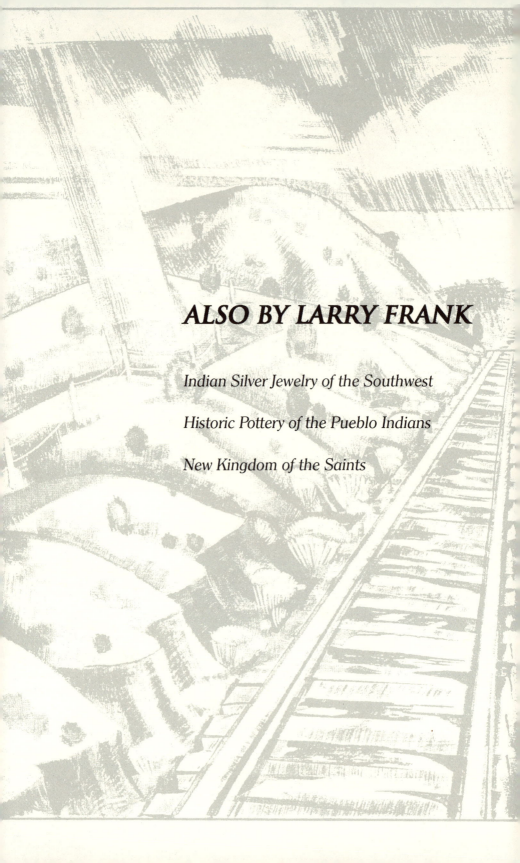

ALSO BY LARRY FRANK

Indian Silver Jewelry of the Southwest

Historic Pottery of the Pueblo Indians

New Kingdom of the Saints

train stops

stories by larry frank

SUNSTONE PRESS
SANTA FE

THIS IS A WORK OF FICTION.
Names, characters, places and incidents either are the product of the author's imagination or are used fictitiously. Any resemblance to events or persons living or dead is entirely coincidental.

Jacket Illustration by Tony Abeyta

© 1998 by Lawrence P. Frank. All rights reserved.

Printed and bound in the United States of America. No part of this book may be reproduced in any form or by any electronic or mechanical means including information storage and retrieval systems, without permission in writing from the publisher, except by a reviewer who may quote brief passages in a review.

Sunstone books may be purchased for educational, business, or sales promotional use. For information please write: Special Markets Department, Sunstone Press, P.O. Box 2321, Santa Fe, New Mexico 87504-2321.

FIRST EDITION

10 9 8 7 6 5 4 3 2 1

Library of Congress Cataloging in Publication Data:
Frank, Larry.
  Train stops : stories / by Larry Frank.-1st ed.
      p. cm.
  ISBN: 0-86534-273-3
  I. Title.
PS3556.R33426T7   1998
813'.54-dc21   98-19308
                                               CIP

Published by   SUNSTONE PRESS
                 Post Office Box 2321
                 Santa Fe, NM 87504-2321 / USA
                 (505) 988-4418 / *orders only* (800) 243-5644
                 FAX (505) 988-1025

*TO MY WIFE, ALYCE,
WHO SHARED THESE STORIES WITH ME*

CONTENTS

PREFACE / 9

VANISHED / 11

TRAIN STOPS IN YOUR MIND / 18

INTO THE PIT / 24

THE DAUGHTER / 40

BLACK AND WHITE / 48

IN LOVE'S DOMINION / 59

THE LAMB AND THE WOLF / 69

CHARGED AND COMBUSTIBLE MOVEMENT / 77

THE MASTER / 84

FINAL DECLENSION / 94

COWS / 98

CAUGHT / 109

QUIET / 116

REHEARSAL / 123

THIRD WORLD ENCOUNTER / 130

THE BAVARIAN CAPER / 135

LOST IN THE SAGEBRUSH NOWHERE / 143

THE DIGNITARY / 149

TURF / 162

THE CAGE / 167

EACH DAY I HUNT / 171

PREFACE

FOR HALF MY LIFE I HAVE LIVED IN A small village just north of Taos, New Mexico, in high desert country of cottonwoods, cedars and piñon trees, all powered by a mesmerizing mountain, studded with ponderosa pine, Douglas fir and aspen. I brought my Los Angeles life with me to a realm crossed with Indian, Hispanic and even Anglo cultures. The scene was a ferment, to me a series of catalysts.

In my early life I wrote and directed films; in my later one I directed plays, wrote poetry, three art books and now, short stories. These are a melange of my old and new selves, first about my childhood and experiences abroad and then in the new land, stories concerning the native Southwest, the land's preservation, people who live in mole holes and fantasy mixed with the real; a packrat's nest of oddities and bits of existence.

Always I tried to have the stories pulsate like changes that course through nature and the heart of man, the dreadful and sweet elements of their make-up, turning into unexpected endings, new twists, a virtual run of train stops, bustling with an array of new patterns and combustibles. What one sees is not always in perfect harmony, with solutions soothing to mind and heart, but rather a journey which enters into hidden and untrackable territory. I like stories that incorporate the truths of old tales and yarns which captivate and educate some mythical audience, stories that resonate with a rich glow of feelings, desire, passion, so palpable that one can savor them like piñons roasted in a fire.

These are the realities and restraints I accept, and I hope the reader gets snagged, carried on by the whirlpool of their conflicts and surfaces refreshed and enriched.

*The earth shifts, impacts upon itself,
sifts;
mountains wear away by fractions,
tear;
the sea lies fallow in itself,
dries;
the sun flumes upon its core,
consumes;
the heart fickles freely,
apart.*

VANISHED

I OFTEN THINK ABOUT IT. GRANDPA and I sharing an experience that still holds me in its grip. Even though the event happened when I was eleven, and I've now been away at college for four years, it gives me a great glowing feeling to cherish what has passed. It changed Grandpa into a different person. He has settled down quiet now because of what took place.

Hominy, Oklahoma is Grandpa's town and where I was born. I lived in a frame house and went to a frame school house that wasn't much. When I was young, I played with the farmers' kids, plus a few Indian children. Nothing exciting came up, except that once a year the town folk would celebrate the founding of Hominy, and that was an event. A big band that sparked a parade of public-spirited citizens would rumble down Main Street tooting, puffing and at times making noises like a squeaking wagon axle. Another group, dressed up to portray famous characters who once coursed through the town's history-explorers, pioneers, trappers, generals-followed the band. Then came the best riders on the best horses one could dream about. They were so beautiful. The horses side-stepped on the street and reared up on their hind legs, snorting, eyes bulging; it was what I'd like to call a splendid celebration.

For the occasion my mother made the best eats that any mother could possibly make, spurred on by the participation of my grandpa, who praised her cooking. The whole affair centered on my grandpa, who had come to town to perform his duty.

My brother Jake, eight years older than I and good looking, had conjured up the notion of marriage to a young female he had known for two years. Jake was Grandpa's favorite grandchild, and the old man wanted to inspect Jake's intended to see if she would be to his liking. Grandpa had asked me what I thought of her and I couldn't describe my impression. On the several occasions I had met her, she had remained silent. When I addressed her, she uttered not one single word. Except once. I overheard her say the word "excruciating." Upon that bit of empirical observation, I came to the conclusion that she was brilliant.

However, Grandpa's passing judgment on Jake's fiancée created a special problem. Every year when the town band would present itself, growling and blaring, Grandpa would also be growling and blaring, quite drunk, producing a little band of noises and antics all his own. No one could predict how Grandpa would react, whether he would be zippy and fiery or kindly and peaceful.

The night of Grandpa's arrival, Jake, his girl Melinda and I were sitting in the living room of my parents' house, the two of them nestling comfortably together. With creamy skin and the longest brown hair that went almost all the way down to her calves, Melinda was a couple of years older than my brother. She looked better than whipped cream. With more than the weight of gravity Grandpa crashed into our fragile group. We could tell by his noisy, sloppy ramblings that he was steaming drunk. Snarly and charged like a locomotive, he burst into the room, wearing a white stubble beard and black preacher-like suit. Melinda just popped up from her seat and out of Jake's arms.

"She looks like a bleating lamb running in circles," he croaked, "white and fleecy as the clouds. But a real eye-catcher, comforting to the eye."

"You be easy on her, Grandpa. You don't be scaring her," Jake said in a flat, scrawny voice.

"You whittled your eyes real sharp to stab a beauty. She's all that, I grant you. And her hair's rich as a beaver's pelt and there's enough to keep you warm in the coldest winter. Why, birds can nest there."

"Now, Grandpa," Jake said, "look at your own scrubby white hair and big red nose–ain't that a sight. At your age you're about as useless as one of those Indians we used to read about in story books. What right do you have badgering poor Melinda?"

"True," he nodded, his head bobbing slowly like a bird sipping water. "Indians used to be my friends, but you can't find them no more. They're gone. But me–I'm just like an old oak tree–I weather well. But this lady, what's her name?"

"Melinda," he answered.

No longer quite as drunk as when he first barged in, Grandpa now had turned sassy and cagey.

"This Melinda, she looks a bit smarter than you, Jake, with a few more years of wisdom on you."

"Yes, she's got me by two years," Jake affirmed.

"You'll never catch up with all her ways. She'll always have a head start on you. Why, you're bound to lose the race–miss the parade."

"Why, Grandpa, there's no race," Jake reflected.

"Not with you always just standing still. If you marry for pretty, you'll never move. I wouldn't blame you. Now you, Melinda, can you milk a cow?"

"No, sir."

To my surprise she actually spoke.

"Can you saddle and ride a horse?"

"No, sir."

"Can you feed pigs and chickens?"

"No, sir."

"Good cook?"

"No, sir."

"Good housecleaner?"

"No, sir."

"Sewing?"

"No, sir."

"Well, any damn fool can see that you should marry her, Jake, real quick!"

Jake was flustered and looked at me. Grandpa sure put Melinda in a pickle.

"Maybe he shouldn't marry me," Melinda spoke firmly.

I was dumbfounded. To me that was the best ever, even better than when she said "excruciating." This was her peak performance. Melinda was sticking up for herself and getting back at Grandpa.

At that moment my mother entered the house, saw what was happening and instantly dragged Grandpa out of the room. The trial was over.

It was generally decreed by my family that Grandpa lined up against Melinda and didn't want this marriage to take place. But the next day at lunch, when he was immaculately sober, he completely changed face and was as quiet and docile as a church mouse, sweet with contentment, even giving her little nibbling compliments. In this case, since the family needed Grandpa's verdict on this crucial matter for its proper operation, his acceptance of Melinda threw us into profound confusion. What did he think? How could we proceed in such a muddle? Everything was up in the air. And all this trouble just before the parade.

The morning of the parade bustled into being and claimed our attention. Grandpa arose early and with unbridled energy woke up the rest of us. For the parade he had been chosen to play the role of an army scout on the alert for the heathen Indian, which he thought was funny because he considered himself the worst heathen around. So we dressed him in an old uniform with some frayed buckskin trimmings to make him look a bit bedraggled, as if he had skirmished with some redskins. We wolfed down our food and hustled out of the house. I managed to slip away unnoticed because I didn't want to be cramped by any of them.

The booming band was impressive enough. The brass instruments shone in the early morning sun and an old army veteran blew a small World War I trumpet. The high school band had joined with the community band, but you could tell which was which because the students made most of the mistakes. Sounding like a charge of artillery, the drummer of an enormous drum huffed and puffed and beat a small hole in one of its sides. The white feathers perched on the tops of the band members' hats fluttered in the wind.

Grandpa marched off with the other performers in the historical parade, towering over a bantam size general who was all but incapable of giving orders to anyone, let alone to Grandpa.

The cavalcade of horses, crackling with energy, resembling the steeds of chivalrous knights, delighted everyone, including the barking dogs. Whatever beauty is, I believe it is caught in the free flow of horses gracing the world. That's it. The parade ended with the last group of horsemen passing by.

But apparently the parade had not ended. Just before noon, when the sun was directly overhead, Grandpa detected an unscheduled newcomer some distance away. Out of the prairie a lone horseman on an exquisite pony slowly emerged from the hot, dusty, red earth. In the harsh bright light his figure was hard to make out, but he was not one of us-no cowboy type from the West. He hardly seemed to move; his horse took tight, springy steps, barely advancing. He gave us the impression of some dark warning about to visit us. Then it burst upon the crowd who he was-an old timer whose time they figured had long been over. It was an Indian, an Indian alone from nowhere or somewhere, who had entered unseen, uninvited, almost unknown, and perhaps unwanted. Grandpa thought he had known him as a boy, but no one had seen an Indian for many years.

The warrior stopped for a moment, waited and then went on. The rider took on the color of the carmine earth. He wore a beaded vest over a buckskin shirt and buckskin pants with beaded leggings and moccasins. Some eagle feathers were tied in his hair. I owned a few feathers from a dead eagle I had found on the road. They were the similar. A hairbone choker encircled the man's throat. His mount, a roan, carried itself and its master proudly; they could not be separated. The horse was resplendent with a beaded martingale, saddle blanket and crupper. A pair of beaded and quilled saddle bags hung on each side of the blanket. The horse's tail was specially bobbed with feathers attached to it.

The Indian stood out from us, a lost individual who long ago had played a part in the backwaters of our history. But his image forced me to bring the past into the present, to sort out the tattered memories that my people had long ago hidden in ignorance and neglect, memories that disturb our peace. We had buried in our minds a kingdom of our own ancestors, of a race that once upon a time had its own words and thoughts and customs.

The warrior still distant, unchanging and distinguished, had dropped the reins and allowed them to go slack, letting the beast carry him effortlessly on his exodus out of our lives. He was leaving those past Indian centuries and heading out on a long trip to the earth's end-to vanish. He might have been a Ponca or a Wichita or a Pawnee. Perhaps he was an Osage or an Oto. I'll never know.

Breaking my trance I became aware of sadness spreading over us. I cried out futilely, mostly to myself, "He is the last Indian, forever going away. That's what he is. Doesn't anyone understand?" Then I saw Grandpa crying, crying in his beard and down his shirt, totally stricken by a grief that shook him apart. He knew! Grandpa started to sway back and forth and broke into a crazy dance that wasn't really so crazy. He was in control and not drunk, but his arms went flying all around and his feet moved in a stutter of broken steps. It made no sense. But no one noticed. The pasts of both Grandpa and the Indian had touched.

Grandpa stopped and froze. He saluted the Indian. The Indian in turn glided before us, bent down and touched Grandpa with his quirt. I could see his profile closely as he passed by: his braided black hair, high cheek bones, strong curved nose and bristling eyes. I was now staring at his back and the horse's rump, the creation of man and animal moving away from where I stood. As if he was a foreigner but special to our parts, he disappeared. I felt an eternal loss. We could never retrieve him.

Quiet had settled over the streets and the family directed its steps home. Jake ambled ahead with Melinda, making sure that she wasn't left alone with Grandpa. Grandpa and I lagged behind. We didn't say anything and he walked with his head down, scrutinizing every stone and stick on the ground.

I looked at Grandpa and felt sad. All of a sudden I realized he wouldn't always be around, and he seemed to know it, too. "It's not only the last Indian," he mumbled. "For both of us our day has come. This day is my last celebration. I'll never come here again. For me there are no more glories."

He and I fell into the same gait and step like we were twins, and he took my hand and held it as we continued homeward. I think from then on Grandpa liked me better than Jake.

TRAIN STOPS IN YOUR MIND

IT WAS DEVOID OF DESTINY. TRACKS SPUN OUT, probing in front of the engine but in alignment with the blustering, hotly pursuing machine that coursed on, swerving, climbing and shooting across lands waiting to be dissected. The train had no decision to make. A woman sat alone by the window. She concentrated on the glass, watching herself in its reflection. Beyond the pane myriad images begged for her attention but fell away in vain. She was intent on capturing the mirrored face cast before her. I am Courtney Morehead, she thought, caught on the surface, fragmented by a background of a changing commentary of visuals that seem to define me, but do not; yet I am still Courtney Morehead. Sometimes, she figured, it would be nice not to be Courtney Morehead, not to drag her prematurely gray hair around at thirty-six, not to bestow her cloudy green eyes wearily on many unsettling scenes. But she realized that even if she changed her name or dyed her hair, she could not avoid bumping into Courtney Morehead. Ouch! She pressed her pointed nose against the window and her breath altered its clarity. She could not make her nose shorter because it came back the same. As a girl, she pushed her nose back and up for hours at a time, but it never changed. Now it pleased her. He, the original and once lovely one, Grady, she recalled, tickled this nose and remarked that it swept upward to a graceful landing strip "where gracious creatures like butterflies and ladybugs could land." No, she could not really change her life's pattern because she lacked the power to do so. She was held captive to the mesmerizing, rushing train, with its wheels grinding down her resistance to what she might face-many fields, hills and streams down the line. She peered out into the early morning and her eyes caught a herd of half black and half white cows. The crazy patchwork of harlequin bovines stared back through the window. He, her current lover, she remembered, liked cows, singled them out as "standers" or "sitters." These were "standers." He liked her, also. Outside, a huge floating weeping willow, crowned by a hawk, passed swiftly by, dragging its green tips on the ground. She sensed she had seen that tree before, perhaps in a cranny of her childhood. No matter. She must get organized. She was going to one of her men, was permanently leaving the other. Yes, confusion. He, her new lover, was waiting. Soon they would meet. As for her estranged husband, she was putting miles and miles of distance between them. On each end of an imaginary line was one of these two men. She had married, barely. Nothing changed between them. She's a goddess to him: passive sex, feigned boredom, unfortunately no children. There were good moments, too-real sparks between them. He was delightfully young and playful, and his teasing banter sweetly engulfed her. Yet he could be stubborn. Whatever happened between them managed always to hurt him. Too late now to make amends. Dark blobs of stunted ducks bobbled on the immense aquamarine lake before her. They were coots. Immobile, they seemed to linger endlessly. Wherever he, her new friend, was, she contemplated, on the bus or in the factory, he would bring his field glasses, strapped over his shoulder just in case he could track any kind of bird through his high-powered lens. One time in Los Padres National Park, he was peering through his glasses when a huge California condor lost its updraft and dropped down right into his field of vision. Seeing this enormous, hideous relic of a prehistoric monster blown up in front of him, he almost had a heart seizure from shock and fright. After that trauma, he carefully manned his binoculars every morning for the visual catch of the day. Funny man. When the train finishes its run in four hours, he will come swinging in from the station, perhaps without his binoculars, and pour searing kisses down on her. He came on strong. But he could be subtle, too. His foreplay was delightful. He would open their lovemaking by walking his two longest fingers down what he called "love's land," across her stomach, stopping at her belly button to rest, then marching over her thighs and ending at the "sheltered oasis." Then they would begin. A whimsical touch. A blast of the train's whistle interrupted her reverie. Looking out, she found the train crossing a high trestle overlooking a muscular whitewater river. A rash of obtrusive boulders studded it. Her intractable husband, she recalled, frequently left her for the river that she couldn't tolerate to share with him. He took countless rafting trips, and when he returned all he did was blather about how frothy white the whitewater was and how he had conquered it, replete with its monolithic crags. Perhaps the river was competing for Grady; she resented it as her main rival. Pretty dumb to blame the river. Had she become less attractive to him during their eight years together? She worried that when he finds out she is gone, he won't think enough of her to try to get her back. He will probably be relieved when she has become another man's problem. The day she booked this train with her travel agent (also a friend of his), Grady had dumped her and was winding his way down the Snake River, simultaneously wearing down any sex urge he might have managed. What a waste. Why couldn't he have a mistress, or even a friendly secretary, to occupy his attention? She certainly did not succeed in turning him on, although she tried. The crisp afternoon sunlight frayed and darkened as Courtney passed through an industrial town with active, intrusive smoke stacks. What villainy! He, her new love, she recollected, owns a factory like this; that's where she met him. She was called to see him about a decorating job to refurbish his office, which was complete with silly male ego furnishings-a stack of trophies and ribbons (he had been a good high school debater), a football signed by an important athlete, a motorcycle helmet and a model ship stuck in a glass box. She told him she couldn't do the job, and anyway, there was no use to brighten up his office when the place looked so dirty. He laughed and called her the "master of the obvious." "All right," he conceded, "just give me a personal decorating job. I can use a little sprucing up." She did that; fine tuned him and made him glow and sing. Meanwhile, she managed to redecorate his office with fresh male trappings. She had bought him duck decoys, an old brass telescope, a globe of the eighteenth century world on a rich wooden stand, prints of fish and horses and some ancient tools, used for obscure purposes, but which featured bold contemporary shapes. She also allowed him to keep his model ship. Breaking her thought, she abruptly noticed the irritating rattling of the cars as they clattered on their rails. Why all of a sudden now? She had begun to feel excited and impatient. She had neatly shed one of her men and was about to confront the other. But dusk always affected her with longing and regret, dragging her back to the past. Lost, she seemed as if she were strapped onto a giant careening body, going fast without direction, carrying her powerlessly onward. She was heading into the inevitable, one way or the other, toward the man who wanted her and was waiting for her, and yet for the first time she had doubts. She had started a chain of events that she was bound to follow. How could she get off the train now? It slowed down and moved tentatively through a line of suburban towns sprinkled with lights. One after another, with no separate identity, the towns joined together. However, each neighborhood formed a small realm of its own, with its town hall, sports stadium, bank, movie theater and church. Her flame, she projected, was planning to buy a house in an area like that. When she was free, they would marry and she could decorate the new house in a style reflecting both their tastes. When she first met him, she figured he was the type who belonged with a house, children, a dog and a wife. He was that pleasant. Only he didn't have any of these. Once he had a wife but divorced her. But now Courtney had to concentrate. On the train platform people were waiting to greet the passengers, some dressed stylishly and holding flowers. She wondered what he, her loved one, would wear. This was the last stop before he would take her away. She did not want to leave just yet; she felt secure in her seat. But she must get ready. She placed her hat on her head, then reached for her two small suitcases and put them on the empty seat beside her. The train came to a complete halt. The passengers put away their dull masks and replaced them with animated expressions. A man abruptly crowded her, blocking the aisle.

"Where do you think you're going, Mrs. Grayhair?"

In shock, she knocked off her hat. "Grady! Where did you come from? What are you doing here?"

"I came to find you–to stop you from running away–to take you home."

"How did you know where to find me?"

"I canceled my rafting trip, and when I checked with the travel office, Oliver told me you had made reservations on this train. I then planned to intercept you just before your destination. I decided I'd better rescue you before it was too late and you had met whoever you are going to see."

"It won't work, Grady. I am not coming back."

"Bullshit! I know about your tire manufacturer. At first I was hurt and stayed away from you, hoping that somehow this agony would end, but it didn't. I was miserable. I couldn't force myself to go on any more river trips, and then I came to my senses and decided to give up the river god for good. I sure have been pig-headed." As he lightened up, he grinned at her and said, "And now I intend to be pig-headed about you. What I want is you, Courtney Morehead. So I've come to get you."

"No, she stammered, "it's too late for that." Suddenly she stopped, as her cheeks colored and her mood changed. She looked up at him amazed and said, "Did you call me 'Mrs. Grayhair'? You called me that name? 'Mrs. Grayhair'?"

"Too late?" he said. "No, it is never too late. Yes, I called you that name. Gray is my favorite color and represents my one and only woman. And I'm fighting to keep that woman."

He quickly picked up one of the bags on the seat and, grabbing the shoulder strap of the other, carried them away.

"No!" she shouted, "give me my bags," but she knew her voice was hollow. She smiled inwardly and thought, he came for me! He broke away from the spell of the cursed river to take me back. He really wants me.

He stopped, looked impudently at her and walked back toward her. With his free hand he took her hand in a vice-like grip and pulled her off the train.

"Let's go and get your hair dyed," he teased. "Then we'll eat at a good restaurant, perhaps take a look at the fine museum here, get a hotel room and make great love all night."

She followed him because he had the exuberant strength and sure direction she had never seen in him before, and because it was inevitable.

INTO THE PIT

I

THE WATER FELT GOOD, WARM AND even soft as it curled around us. A weak tide ran, lapping gently against our bodies, and it lifted us slowly up and down. The white sand was now gray and the sun, half set, lingered, not finished with its spell. I made long ballet leaps as the swells gracefully buoyed me up and then gradually settled me back down. Moving up I hit the egg yolk sky and it ran all over me, squeezing me down into the warm water, leveling me off so the sea could kiss the sky cleanly.

Mari paddled far from the shore toward the melting horizon line, now filtering into the night. Her little head, bobbing like a cork, piloted her. She would swim like a cat in a fight, churning the water, and then rest or satisfy some curiosity and wait for me. She didn't need to call this time; I came to her. She would not exactly hold onto me but our bodies would stick together, causing a warm suction, my back supporting her softness. The waves were larger now and we pounded through them, heading home. I could see the swells rear and slap my head and splatter down the bridge of my nose.

We could barely make out the beach, but we knew where our possessions were on the rocks. The water was everywhere, flanking a ribbon of beach and surrounding on three sides a rocky ridge that lined the way to the towering cliffs. We scrambled onto a rock and surveyed our faded orange sleeping bag (meant for only one person), two bottles of water and some bread and fruit. We had secured the food and water from the city on the empty cliffs behind us. The Italian kid who brought us to the beach on a tub of a boat promised us more if I would give him some cigarettes. I had extras, which I gave him.

Mari told me to roll out the sleeping bag but it wasn't even since the middle part sagged into a depression. Feeling a particularly rocky spot, I said to her, "I hope you're well padded tonight; you'll need to be. I never saw a girl before who always wanted to do things in the most difficult way. Here we could have had a nice hotel with a warm bed and a bath, good food, no work or effort. But not you–you didn't want that. You have to find some hole of a beach to starve and die in. And I already paid American Express for a room–for two nights."

She saw that I was laughing and she giggled aloud. Her smile and laugh were her. You didn't notice much else, because she wasn't there with you until her cheeks rose up to her small chiseled nose that wrinkled a little and her delicate mouth opened slightly. And it didn't much matter what she said because you knew that she was happy or at least playing, and so what counted was how she played, how she bubbled and chirped her feelings.

"You can go back to your wealthy friend Walter if you want to," and she moved her head sharply from side to side, her long golden hair touching her shoulders. "You can have him. Oh, yes, he's so interesting and intelligent, too. He's just fine for you. You do as you like," she teased.

"Listen, Mari, I came with Walt all the way to Europe. We were supposed to stick together, and just because a silly, saucy little Frenchy came between us, I don't know how . . . . "

I started laughing again because it was so funny–Walt in the nice hotel, wandering around the city, keeping to himself, eating tasteless American food wherever he could find it, and mostly sleeping. I tried to keep my face serious but only partly succeeded. "Walt's my friend and I don't want to hurt him."

Mari was partially listening, and when she heard my voice stop she looked at me and smiled understandingly. Her smile seemed that way; all she felt and shared was in it. I have often wondered what Mari felt. She liked to play with words, phrases, smatterings that we had talked about countless times, and she would continually arrange them in new, attractive ways. And she would often add original twists, intonations, perhaps even interpretations of the same themes. These favorites were the sheen of her emotions, and when she was content or made love she would return to the same themes; in fact, she would never really leave them.

She took her clothes out of the duffel bag and sidled up to me. The speckled tide returned to start again; it rolled with ancient regularity. Mari began her rhythms of play in minion tones.

"I know all about that, about Walter. You know me, Love, you know what kind of girl I am. I'm not like the other girls-I don't like what they like, to gossip, to care only about material possessions, to do unimportant things-you know that."

"I know, Mari."

I slid my hands over her compact body. Like water her body flowed together with her breasts banked gracefully above; no big Rhine maiden with gross enlargements.

"No," she agitated, "not now. I just want to be with you. You know that I prefer to be here with you on the beach, not any beach but a special beach, instead of up there with all those boring people. They're not interesting." Her face was one of controlled smiles.

"I know you, Darling."

"No, I told you. Not now. I don't feel like it. Stop."

She squirmed away and began getting out the food. The bread was good with the little bit of chocolate that she had hoarded. We became familiar again. The good sensation from the food warmed us.

"What about the Swiss, Mari?" I threw out.

"Oh, the Swiss, they're great people," she teased, "just like the Swiss Navy that won the war. That's all they talk about, how much water's in their lakes.

They're almost as passionate as the English."

"Well, what about the land of Italy? Here we are in beautiful Sorrento with a starry sky and you and me and love."

She cautioned herself a moment. "I don't know. I don't know the Italians, but I don't trust them. They've got Latin blood like the French-they're exciting, but . . . . "

"But they're not Frenchies. You Napoleon bloodsuckers-you have nationalism in your milk."

"Oh, the Americans, they just chew their tongues like dumb cows and mix sardines with cocoa." She distorted a smile. "The dumb Americans, they're not civilized. Like you-you chew your tongue."

I took a gulp of weird green from the water bottle. It looked like a miniature sea.

"Seriously, Mari, I'm serious now. I don't like that guy who's supposed to run the place here, waking us up last night, trying to rent us a cabin. He was too persistent; he practically climbed into the bag with us. It was a good thing my shorts were on or he would have seen a perfect specimen of a man," I joked. "This morning he and another fellow were rowing around these rocks looking supposedly for sea shells or something, exactly when they shouldn't have, when I was taking pictures of you. Well, I took them anyway. And I know he was showing off when he was displaying his canoe everywhere a few hours ago."

She began her inventions-having her deadly serious fun. "And . . . . "

"He's always looking at us, at you. He won't go away."

"And . . . . "

"I'd watch him closely; I think he's dangerous."

"Oh, I think you're mad, I really do. But, oh, Todie, would you protect me with all your strength, your small shoulders, everything you have, if I was in danger? You would help me, just like you give me affection and tenderness and love. I know I can trust you."

"You know I would, Mari."

"I know."

She was quiet and tenderly lovely. The stars arranged themselves like hard glinty mica bits. They formed a neatly fitting roof resting firmly on the encircling cliff walls. The waves drowsily crept to the rocks and clung to them. Occasionally, a current would sting the blackness making short slaps below us. We were alone with each other, very much alone.

"I don't want you tonight," Mari snapped. "Anyway, you haven't shaved and you're not clean. I don't like you that way. You're not smart-looking."

"That's silly. I'm as clean as you."

"Anyway, my back hurts from the sun. You should have put more oil on me. I burn."

"Hell, you roasted yourself like a greasy little porker wallowing in the sand."

"I'm tired and I'm going to sleep now. You can do what you want. I'm going to wear this slip in case anyone comes, like last night."

"I'll go in with you. I'm tired, too."

We wiggled into the too-small bag, practically snaking it off the rock. This was not a soft, mossy rock. I squeezed in hard against Mari and let her absorb the vivid images crowding in around me. Mari spoke of that night we had in Rome, "when I first saw that you were a lover and mine," but I couldn't play on with her because it was too much work and I was following a pattern of stars stringing into the sea. I kissed her with little kisses on her neck. When I looked at the stars sailing crazily, I sang half aloud (for Mari to hear) some words I had rhymed to a favorite tune:

"Gods above me,
Do you love me?
Please don't shove me
Into the pit."

Mari turned and bumped me. "You talk like a book. Don't say that! You know how I don't like you when you make fun of serious things. You shouldn't do that."

"I know. Bonsoir, my petite Mari."

"You'll never learn how to speak French," she said.

II

I WOKE UP SLEEPING ON MY BACK.
Two darker-than-night figures hovered above us. They were poking the bag with their feet or a stick and talking in low tones to each other. Mari and I saw them at the same time in the thick blackness. We squeezed tighter together, hoping they would go away. Feebly, we tried to sit up but flopped sideways; we were strait-jacketed. The men were smaller than I am, with thick torsos and dark skins. One had no shirt; they both had no shoes. They motioned us to get up. I grappled with the ties of the bag and we wiggled free. One of them got to the side of me and the other faced me, a long curved shepherd's staff in his hand.

"Venite con noi alla polizia."

Mari was afraid. I tried to reassure myself by holding her waist. "I think he wants to take us to the police. There's no police around here. What did we do?"

She sucked in her breath. "Ask them why."

"Perche?" I asked. "La polizia?"

The other man was clawing through our belongings but stopped, leaving them scattered.

"Venite con noi alla polizia!" the first man repeated and shoved Mari and me towards the beach. I grasped Mari and we stuck to our rock like bleating sheep.

Mari clutched me tightly as the men pulled at her shoulders and waist. She suddenly let go and pleaded desperately, "Noi ... dormire ... signora, no signora e signor ... soli ... comprendere?"

She spoke in a fitful jerking rhythm. "Todie, don't leave me, don't let them separate us!"

One man wedged in and cut us in half. The other yanked Mari's shoulders back and lifted her away. Yet we came back to each other, finding the way through the net of their hands. The first man raised a stick and cocked it above his head, making soft clubbing motions. He had no more patience; he had no need for it. He stared at Mari and said to his friend, "La ragazza, alla piaggia." They had herded us nearly off the rock.

Mari's mind bolted. "They're taking me to the beach-they want me. Todie, they're going to rape me! Don't let them separate us!" She faced them. "Io signora, egli signor, noi, dormire, comprendere?" She was half-crying and heaving spasmodically. Her body's warmth gave me the reassurance of her importance, that she's mine and this trouble would go away.

Mari was mine, she was a part of me and she was being destroyed-unraveled. She was sadly pretty now; she had belonged to me so happy. I looked at the men. I thought of escape and rescue, of the waiting sea and of the water-splattered rocks below, of the muscle-filled man, his stick and horrid black death. Mari was in danger and it was me against two men. I braced my feet to stop their momentum and begged, "Prego, prego, prego, Signori!"

We were off the rock now, stumbling and falling on stones. Mari screamed, "Don't kill him!" as I slipped and struggled. The front man tried to gag Mari with his short thick hands and then he rubbed her smooth slip to feel her body. The man in back with the stick was pushing me and threatening to smash me. Mari made some loud gnarled sound which he muffled. I could get no help from atop the powerful cliffs or along the stretches of sand. They only echoed "signora e signor" and "prego," gently fading, lost. I wanted Mari with everything I had; I loved her then. Each rock led to another with water syruping between. They finally shoved us onto the sandy beach. One said, "La signora prima, alla polizia," and he took Mari away into the dark. I heard her shriek, "Todie, don't do anything; they'll kill you!"

I moved toward the crouching, waiting menace, whining my conviction. "You know there aren't any police-you know there aren't. Prego-la signora!"

Everything waited. I thought I saw something shiny like a knife, glistening in his hand. Mari was being mutilated and I could do nothing because a man was stopping me. Frantic, I walked stiffly up and back; the slushy sand soothed my cut feet. He smiled and laughed at the waste of effort.

It took only five minutes before the first man returned. He came swiftly, alone, a relay runner passing burning words to his relief. The second received the muted directions he already knew and disappeared. The first man faced me and said nothing and did nothing but mark the time. When he received a call from his friend, he nonchalantly relaxed his hold on the stick, jumped up and ran down the beach. I followed. My feet kicked out high and easy in the surf, and then I came to Mari. The men were looking at her, friendly, curiously, observing her as unreal, deformed, wondering what she would do next. Mari, in her slip, twisted up from the sand, low to the ground and fell into me.

"Oh, Todie, they have hurt me!" She was richly sobbing.

I held her up under her arms, her hands working my back, her knees dragging in the sand. "Darling, please try to get hold of yourself. Please!"

The men were silent and stood there. Then one put out his hand. "Arriverderci." I shook it. "Arriverderci." They stepped back for a few seconds and then went their way.

I helped Mari to the sea's edge because it was easier to walk there, although the waves splashed her slip.

"Let's hurry, Darling Mari, as far away as we can. What did they do to you? Oh, my Sweetheart!"

Waves of fresh cold were injected through me as my toes squished into the wet sand. Mari calmed; the night seemed to have transformed her. She withdrew her hand from mine and stopped, stooping slowly to lift up her slip.

"I think I'll wash here. I don't want anything to happen and I think the salt water will stop everything. I don't have anything else."

She was sad and solitary, like a cat licking its body clean.

When we reached our rock, I noticed that it wasn't so big and secluded as I had thought, but like the others, invaded and taken by wind and water and man. It was very cold for both of us and yet our tired bodies began to relax. Mari shivered and got inside the bag. She rested while I guarded her.

"Mari, I feel so bad because I love you and I just stood there and did nothing, nothing at all. I just let everything go and I wanted to give you everything. I was afraid."

"I know, my Todie. I was, too. I understand. There was nothing you could have done. He had a stick and would have hurt you. I want a live lover, not a dead one. You love me and that is what's important. This has brought us closer together."

I was consuming her clumsily with kisses, and I flopped her like a doll. "My Maria, I . . . . "

"Do not call me Maria, never again! It's a common name here. I'm your Mari!"

"I'm sorry, I won't."

"What did I tell you? I don't trust the Italians. They're beasts, not honest- I know."

"They're not all like that."

"I know them. This is the first time I have ever been raped-nothing has happened like this-not like this!"

I thought about what Mari had told me once, that at thirteen she was attacked by a young French student from a good family intimate with her own. She was left in his care for the evening by the joint families. Mari never told. She was sick for a long time after that.

"It was worse when your friend wronged you, especially when you were so young, when he took advantage of you. It was much worse."

"It's not the same thing," she said.

I could not forget; Mari had gone down and I let her be cut through. I did not fight and stop them and it was my fault that it happened. "Mari, are you all right, Darling? Did they hurt you?"

"Oh, it was all right, my Todie. They did not hurt my body, but they hurt the balance I have-my mind. It was like scraping me inside. I tried to fight them at first but they would have forced me and injured me. And I think one of the men was the man who stays on the beach. I would have yelled but there was no use, we were so far away. There was no one else there to help us. They did not do much . . . . "

"They had you, Mari, they had you and they hurt you! We must go to a doctor."

Mari was rifling through our clothes and when she found what she wanted, a silver-covered comb, she looked relieved.

"It could have been worse," she whipped. "You sang that song at God and made fun of Him but He stopped it from being worse. I wasn't ruined for life and none of our things were taken. You are silly to make fun."

"I won't, Mari."

Mari was quiet, touched by sleep, and she smiled at me, a smile of old words with old looks and they rang true to her. "You really do love me. You will take care of me. You know that I was very sad before–I thought of being a nun. Now I have happiness with you. You're my life, my soul. I have nothing without you."

The night is still night until the blackness ends. The dark served as background to set off the disturbing flashes of my mind. Then up from the beach and over the rocks emerged a man with a swinging light. He grew closer and I woke Mari. I stood up into a shock-prepared stance, a water bottle clenched in my hand. Even in the dark Mari first saw his face and recognized him as the manager of the beach. "That's him," she whispered. "If he suspects we know that, he and his friend will try to kill us. But if we are friendly to him he will talk a little and try to rent a cabin to us and then leave us alone. He wants to know if we know."

It was just as she said. He scaled the last rock, bounded across to us and gawked nervously. He offered us a bottle of fresh water and talked about the cabins. We told him we were comfortable and he left via his rocky path.

The rest of the night was miserable. I couldn't find my watch and money and Mari talked about that a lot-what were we going to do. She couldn't fall asleep. I worried about my gear, too-whether the men had stolen it or scattered it. The dark grayed some but it was still night. Two fishing boats with lights attached to their long snout-like stems began filtering in through the rocks. I was feeling uneasy. When I looked at Mari, limp and loosely spread out, she excited me. I heard some voices singing and in the gray dawn I barely made out two women in a boat, washing their hair.

When it was early light I caressed Mari awake. She rubbed her eyes with stubby fingers and asked me if we had to leave so early. We were already dressed so we just had to put all our belongings back in the bags. Mari found the watch and the money belt in the duffel bag and was very happy; being practical was a personal triumph for her. We dragged along, lumped together, across the ridge of rocks leading to the cliffs and I lowered Mari to the dry sand. I looked out over the sea that now would be different; there was the turn of a cycle, the ashen sky of dawn opening. I crowed some tune I liked and Mari smiled and sang, "Mister Todie! My, you have a grand voice today."

I leaped to her and held her tenderly. "Oh, Mari, you adorable girl!"

As we pushed up the dirt road on the side of the cliff to the city above, we were caught by the beach keeper. He yelled to us at the foot of the road and wondered why we were leaving, but we strained and broke away fast to gain the top. The sun was now full out soaking the sea with heat, but now sullied, it wasn't our sun.

III

I PHONED WALT THAT AFTERNOON to explain what had prevented us from meeting him. Although he was sorry for Mari, he still resented the delay. I told him he should meet us at the station and take the train to Florence with us at 9:30 the next evening.

That the police must be informed came to Mari at once. There is the usual procedure in such matters. I told the hotel owner about our fate on the beach. I wished the name of a good doctor and asked him for a nice room with a bath and some lemon or vinegar for Mari. He was quite shocked (it was clearly visible), and he assured me that this had never happened before in Sorrento, and it certainly would not have occurred this time if we had used one of the various beach hotels. He knew the man we mentioned, or thought he knew him, and readily believed our story since the man was probably from Napoli, a city which to him was a receptacle of bad men who lived like lice.

The hotel owner gave us his last room and accompanied us to it, fumbling with apologies. The room was set far back in a secluded portion of the hotel. As he took us farther down the hall, the wallpaper started to fade and wilt and finally to unravel. In the room, Mari glanced around quickly, appraisingly. It was good-sized with cream walls and one iron-framed single bed at each end. The shades did not quite shut out a white spurt of light. Mari immediately pulled them.

"Darling Mari-girl, let me help you!" I rushed to the shades. "I should do that."

She sat on a bed, stirring an idea. "I am your little girl, am I? Todie's little girl."

"You are, Mari," and I began rubbing her, feeling her outline and compressing her with gratification.

"Oh, I must undress now, hurry and bathe, or I will be more hurt."

There was a knock at the door and a boy stood with a hot solution in a pitcher and a pan of boiled water. Mari took them and poured them into the bidet in proper mixtures. She straddled the bidet and washed herself.

"I like hot," she said. "This cleans me," and she assumed a knowing, business-like demeanor. She slapped the water and scrubbed her loins. I enjoyed her movements and carriage. She was surprisingly pretty and fragile in a soft-suffering way and yet assertive, in control.

"I don't want a little Todie, yet. And from him, oh please, no baby badman!"

The beds were far apart so I dragged one across the room to the other, and she got in.

"I can't be with you now, Mari—only one to each bed. I miss you, I want you."

"Do you? Come to me, Todie. I am alone."

I crossed over to her as she was lying on her back, shoulders showing and hair wild. "What do you see?"

"I see a little girl."

"Do you love her?"

"Yes."

"How do you know?"

"A little birdie told me." I waited.

"Todie, Todie, do you lu-uu-ve me?" She took hold of me and shook my neck. Then her nails dotted my arms, while lips hardened and her face became intense, delighting in the ritual.

"I am yours."

She was quiet.

"I want sleep now, Todie-love, Todie-mine. You must go to your bed so I can sleep."

I desperately wished to be with her in a double bed and she sympathized. She extended her hand so I could have it. My whirring mind lapsed. I said, "The French and Latins, they always sleep."

She was asleep.

The hotel owner made arrangements for us to see the police. Mari desired this, I could tell. She wanted justice and I agreed, because the beach keeper was personally repulsive and because he should be punished for what he did. But I–I was not sure he was the man, and I feared myself in the situation. Would I do what they expected of me?

I took Mari to the recommended doctor, who was very prosperous. We passed with priority through a line of less prosperous people sitting in a bright, linoleum-floored room. The doctor examined Mari and said she would soon get well. He would not charge them for this was a stain on the city; it was service gratis–the only honorable thing to do.

We foolishly took an expensive tourist horse carriage to the police station. In a square room were two officials. A short, fleshy, middle-aged man with gray-fringed hair sat at a desk at the room's center. He was almost handsome. His complacent, round face detracted from his kind, fatherly, gray eyes which had a casual absorbing sharpness. Leaning against the wall was a tall, thin, wire-strung man who seemed as if he had remained in his middle thirties for many years. He had an impassive look over his sallow, angular features.

The inspector, the man at the desk, gradually warmed to us. He spoke simple English well and never extended himself beyond that level. General information–that I was a student tourist who, while returning to the States, met Mari, and that Mari was French and now living with her family in Paris–came out gently. Then he asked Mari to give her story. While we talked, the tall man sat down quietly behind us. I don't know if he understood us, but his frame was straight and alert.

Mari sincerely recounted the night. She said that she was here to prevent others from suffering. The inspector asked her if she was positive she had recognized and could identify the offender because it could mean a life sentence for him. He liked Mari and felt a bond of compassion. He spoke a little French with her and gave us gleanings from his life. He was not married.

"I realize that this has been a great shock to you. It is a very serious crime here. You must tell us if you are absolutely certain; we must be correct." He flushed, paternal and grave.

"Oh, I know it was him! I could smell his filthy body. He was the same height and talked the same and I could just see his face. He acted strangely today and the night before. He was wrong and should be punished. Todie-Love," she chirped serenely and confidently, "you saw him take me and hurt me and you know it was him."

I winced. "It was quite dark, Mari–in the middle of the night, asleep, and the rocks and all–it was difficult to tell. I wasn't as close as you and it was black."

"Would you know the other man?" the inspector questioned.

"I should if I could see him again," she affirmed.

"And you?"

"I don't think so–it happened so fast," I blurted.

Mari turned to me and squeezed my hand. "You know he deserves this–he took me by force. What's the matter with you?"

"I let you go down. I left you."

"You couldn't help it. Now everything will be all right."

The inspector nodded at the tall man and slapped his hand on his desk. "We have enough evidence to jail him. Take two cars and this young man to identify him."

I left Mari a kiss and followed the man to the cars. We drove onto the dirt road, a driver, the tall man and myself in a small car with four other members of the police in a sedan to our rear. The car was too low for the tall man and he slumped forward. Whether slumped or standing, his double breasted white linen suit streamed down, collecting folds of material that hung over a fastened button. It gave him a sunken appearance. The rest of him looked neat-a tiny, fine tie knot wedged against his collar and polished black shoes.

We partly slid on rocks down the road to the wooden boardwalk. There were several refreshment stands flocked with people getting drinks and trying to relieve their sweat. The tall man glided fast and effortlessly through, and then I pointed to the beach manager, who had a short solid-packed build. He was filling buckets from the public showers.

"There he is."

I didn't hate him, I thought. It was so dark I could not really know it was him.

The tall policeman acted. His frame of steel snapped back. He seized the manager and, holding a hard object in his fist, busted him in the face and split his skin until it was raised and crinkled. The hurt animal screamed, "Prego! Prego! Perche!", words Mari and I had used in vain that night.

They took him away to the sedan and that was the last I saw of him and the beach. The tall man had not even wrinkled his shirt.

Back in the inspector's office, Mari and I were told that the beach owner had not confessed-perhaps a matter of time. A long, curved stick found in the beach keeper's shack was shown to us and that made me feel better. It seemed somewhat like the original. The inspector asked me if I had actually seen the knife the other man had and I ashamedly said that I was not sure. They didn't find the second man when we were there but they took Mari's address. Both of us thanked the inspector and said good-bye. Mari had talked to him alone for a long time.

"Mari-girl," I asked, "tonight is our last stay here. You're positive that the beach keeper was the man? They're beating him. I feel sorry for him."

"Silly puppy, it's over. He must be the criminal. Anyway, let's not think about it; it's not nice. What is old Walter doing, funny Walter?"

The next morning the hotel owner said the inspector had confirmed his earlier statement that the accused man was from Napoli. We expressed our appreciation for the hotel owner's services and more directly paid him fat piles of lira for expenses. I had just enough lira to ride a carriage to the station and locate Walt on a bench in the small depot, worrying about us. The question was: where do we go from here?

THE DAUGHTER

VERNON, A VENERABLE PAINTER, HAD periodically told Jock about his daughter, an attractive, intelligent, unmarried daughter. Not his only daughter, but a cherished daughter, nevertheless, and his only eligible daughter, which added a special dimension to her attributes.

Jock took a trip to Europe with Vernon and his considerably younger wife to see art of the superstars. They mostly got along. When they saw the Winged Victory at the Louvre, the wife mentioned that her daughter had finished college and was teaching something or other that sounded humanitarian. At the Rodin Museum, viewing the Thinker, Vernon remarked that their daughter was working for some degree in her special chosen field and was doing quite well in her unattached state of being.

"Jock," Vernon said with regularity, "maybe you two should meet. Just meet. There might be something between the two of you. And your age differences are not bad."

They were not bad or good, he figured. They were about ten years apart. So what. They were literally several thousand miles apart, perhaps millenniums or universes apart. It was flattering that one very successful artist and his wife wanted their daughter to marry another successful artist. Success was the basic denominator here. Fine. But what else is there to talk about? Well, there is the snapshot Vernon showed Jock. It revealed a lithe, black-haired woman, sloe-eyed with clean cut features, all respectable but nothing compelling or urgently arresting. Still, decidedly decent looking, Jock had to admit.

In Florence, Michelangelo's David overheard Vernon again casually speak about his unencumbered daughter, as his wife and Jock marveled at the statue. In London, Jock and the monument to Lord Nelson in Trafalgar Square stood stoically among cascading words about the untethered daughter. At long last the trip came to its natural and blessed end, and Jock bid good-bye to his friends, and by proxy their daughter.

Jock worked with huge slabs of wood found in nature-roots, boles, burls, knots, driftwood, fragments found underwater in swamps, struck by lightning or buried in the ground or snow. He was in constant search. Some pieces he found weighed thousands of pounds and took special trucks and equipment to haul back to his shop. Often little had to be done to the natural shape of the wood, but most needed to be cut, trimmed, buffed and polished to reveal their luster and subtle infusions of color. But beyond all else his incandescent zeal was for the right material. The tools he used (as well as his hands) were often battered by the stress they underwent in fashioning the congealed and hardened woods. He had a collection of broken saws and chisels. At times it took months to complete a piece of sculpture. Well known, respected, with little competition, he commanded a good price for his art.

For ten years now he had worked hard and played little. He had no diversions except one: he enjoyed women. They came easy to him. Thirty-five, rugged and distinctly handsome, reasonably bright, and with increasing fiscal clout, women swarmed to him. Once in a crazy, senseless game, he counted fifty he had wooed and conquered, and a few days later, he discovered nine more. There was recently a run of Hispanic ones-waitresses, models, cooks, clerks-that he took to his house and, after the love act, let out. Each instance ended for him pleasantly and predictably. He was amazed at his power and control.

No woman stayed with him longer than a night. They weren't important enough and he was too demanding. For a few hours he was a decent lover, but he couldn't love around the corner and into the next day, when he would drop all pleasurable excursions and resume his exacting profession. Yet he was cognizant that he talked to himself alone, made his bed alone and cooked his meals alone, and that the continuity of female companionship only filled in some of the void. He maintained an elusive balance between his privacy and female relationships. Did he want to decidedly tip the scales in favor of one side or the other?

Then the letter arrived that ruffled his peace. From Vernon, the letter contained two photographs, neither related to the trip they shared together, although they were not entirely unrelated. One was of the daughter and the other of both the daughter and wife laughing. He didn't realize how attractive the mother was, particularly when compared to her daughter. She was a larger, fleshier, more seductive edition, but not quite as refined. Both women elicited his attention.

A note accompanied the photographs. Vernon was commissioning Jock to sculpt a piece for him and to bring it to their home in person. In the spirit of the relationship between him and the family, he decided to accept. Not that it was necessary in order to gain access to their home or that he needed the work. He sensed he had a special task to accomplish, and perhaps in this case a rite of passage.

He immediately went to a lake he knew high in the mountains at timberline around which prehistoric Indians had left flint arrowheads and pot sherds. There he found a huge, burled tree root that had been blasted and burned by lightning and which was now covered by water. This ancient mass had undergone a baptism of fire, earth and water. It was up to Jock to unfold the secrets of its creation. He cut a slab eight inches thick and four feet in diameter. Using scrapers, sandpapers and his own chemical formulas, he removed dark layers of putrefaction. Textures of grain and variegated hues from water stains and mud encrustations emerged until the root revealed itself as a table.

Jock crated the root and drove three days to the small seaside town in North Carolina where Vernon's family lived in a stalwart, white, two-story, wooden Edwardian house. Vernon enthusiastically patted him on the back and with the help of the gardener carried the crate in. The large gathering room was completely covered with luminous seascapes, landscapes and still lifes of the region. Jock thought his table would contribute to this environment.

Vernon's wife, Dossie (he caught her name just in time), entered and received him effusively with a hug and kisses. She was clearly delighted. "The commission," Vernon raised his voice. "I am impatient to see my commission." Immediately they focused on the crate, opened it, disposed of the residue and gasped. There gleamed the wondrous orb, King Arthur's round table or the mystic table of the sun. It resonated beauty.

At that moment, that precise instant, a young woman entered the room. She cried out softly when her dark almond-shaped eyes embraced the table. Vernon glanced in her direction. "The daughter," he pronounced, "the last daughter of the world. Amy, meet Jock."

Everyone was charged with expectation. Amy saw a man she liked instinctively, the creator of a hallowed table. He saw a slight, small-boned delight, with penetrating eyes and thin wispy hair, everything that was intrinsically interesting. She moved into the room and faced him.

"I've looked forward to your visit," she almost whispered. "I have been told about you."

Dossie chuckled. "And he's been told about you, too."

"Well," Vernon smiled, "and happily it all worked. The magic table has spun a spell upon us all and now we live under its enchantment."

They all laughed but wondered if it was not true.

The next day after a family breakfast, Jock and Amy went into the sun porch which fronted the ocean. Over the following days intense talks evolved into prolonged sessions. They were usually alone because Vernon was frequently gone and at times spent the night at his sick aunt's home. Jock was aware that his time with Amy was fleeting, since in a week he had to leave. Each day she wore different clothes, each day she was different. He evolved an open bantering style, new for him. He could even strut for her.

On the first day they were alone she moved close to him and confided, "Ever since my parents first told me about you, I've been intrigued. A man who takes from nature but gives back something even more lovely–you do that. I finger your image in my mind, turning it over and over. But I should explain; you don't know me yet. There's little to tell. I've been busy teaching several classes but I'm restless. Even with all this love from my family, I need more. I sometimes feel consumed by desire. I'm not what I appear to them. Yes, they have been good to me, but I become bored easily. When I'm with them there's a sense of blandness that stifles everything I do. Sometimes I ignore my family and hole up at college and study. When I work hard, even to a point of exhaustion, it gives me a sense of exhilaration. Then I am able to see into all the cracks and crannies, and I see into you–you're always alone. And yet you have lots to share. The table that came out of you, out of your passion–that passion is what I want. There's an invisible link connecting us. I want us to be part of each other."

He replied: "I see that we are similar; we work by ourselves. I respect that you have your own world. For me, every day is full of surprise. Days sometimes crackle with great adventures. I like that. You are a new surprise. And now that you and I have just collided, we should find out more about each other. The days we have here are like chapters. But we should turn the pages slowly."

As if she hadn't heard, she moved into him without hesitation and swarmed him with insistent kisses, covering his face and neck, darting her tongue, running her fingers through his hair. He absorbed her fire, drew her into his wildly beating heart, if not his soul, almost causing her to cry out with pain.

Then she separated from him.

"We might be seen. Tonight," she whispered, "late, at two in the morning, when they are asleep, come to my room. More surprises. The richest chapter!"

◆

His sleep was shredded by excitement. He silently got up a little before the appointed time. It was hopelessly dark and he could only feel his way up the stairs while he slid his hand along the railing. He passed her parents' room, then the bathroom. Her room was next. The stairs slightly reverberated under his steps, but when he reached the hallway the floor boards creaked loudly and he almost turned back, fearing he would be discovered. At one point the noise was unbearable and he even thought the boards were breaking beneath him. He froze for a moment, not daring to take a step. But finally the door, slightly ajar, appeared before him.

Inside he saw her. She was stretched out under the covers and he eagerly joined her. He told her that he had not slept a wink and she said "shhhh" to quiet him down. He'd better be still. She felt incredibly soft. The unexpected: her breasts were prominent and her hips exquisitely sculpted. Her back sped smoothly into her buttocks. Her legs were strong as she encircled him. Even her hair seemed unexpectedly rich as it first tickled and then blinded him. Her stomach contracted and her body glided with marvelous rhythms. She made tiny moans. Nothing went awry.

Jarringly, a door slammed.

"I better go!"

He rolled off the bed, dressed and swiftly disappeared.

He went to breakfast late, grinning broadly, until he saw her face dark with anger.

"Where were you last night? What were you doing? You didn't show up," she fumed. "And you were supposed to be my hero-artist and lover."

Stunned, he said, "What? What did you say?"

"Where were you last night?" she almost screamed. "All I got was an empty bed!"

Hastily trying to make sense of the puzzle and avoiding her question, he quickly asked, "Where are your parents?"

She rasped, "Vernon stayed at his aunt's house and mother is still in her room. What has that got to do with it? Where were you? Answer me!"

Jock snapped, "Stop this!" Then the truth instantly came to him, revealing the disastrous mistake he had made. What a mess, he thought. Now he had to take the offensive. He continued, "You can't control me this way," and he was satisfied with his fierce, strident tone. "You can't just order what you want-the precise angle of love-or the exact calibrations of one's heart beat. It won't work with me. I'm not your perfect prescription. I want you in my way-in my own time. Last night would not have worked anyway. My hernia hurt. But with a dash of romance and a flick of tenderness," he smiled, "I can order it healed."

She softened somewhat. "Oh, a healer! We now have a healer and an artist, to boot. You can simply turn your old hernia on or off. You can dial love on or off. Well, then," she said, relaxing, "I want it on-full blast for me. I waited for you last night. I think I scorched the bed," she teased.

He reached out and fondled her fine, dainty hair. "I'll tell you what. I came here for a peek-a-boo, for a lark, to tickle my curiosity. And I encountered more than I bargained for." With his hands, he acted out his barrage of nonsense. "A black pearl. A six-sided rainbow. A money-sap tree. I unearthed the daughter. Vernon's sweet, dutiful, blessed daughter. No! Rather, I met the underside of a dank stone full of crawly things, the red spot on the black widow's belly, the porcupine's pricks," he purred as he continued to enjoy his catalogue of items, "the giraffe's inaudible cry-all qualities of yours that I admire. Plus, the mysteries. Ah! the unknowable mysteries, and there are plenty. You liked my table, which was my litmus test indicating your feelings for me. You prevailed. Now, because of these imponderables, I am here by providence to ask you to marry me." He laughed, "Let's get hitched."

She turned her head sideways and smiled. "Absolutely I'll marry you but . . . . "

"But what?"

She hesitated.

"What?" he echoed.

"Can we have sex now?"

"Certainly."

"Right now?"

"Certainly."

"Then let me show you the way. I'll make sure you don't get lost."

"Certainly."

BLACK AND WHITE

IT WAS WELL KNOWN THAT JAN Vandergrift had exquisite taste, perfectly honed. Certainly the museum's board of directors considered him infallible. For eighteen years he had industriously acquired treasures for the institution, bringing it national recognition. He felt secure, confident, acutely aware of his blessings. Approaching fifty, he and his wife worked well together. Their friends were wealthy, intellectually stimulating. He earned a sizable salary and relished his profession.

Nevertheless to him the painting hung crooked and was poorly framed; Jan Vandergrift's life was amiss.

One evening Jan and Violetta decided it would be fashionable to stay home and talk to each other. They had just shown three trustees to the door and returned to claim their scotch and sodas. From the French Empire table Jan picked up a Ming Chinese jade figure, fondling it. To Jan, in a pensive mood, the room seemed frozen in a moment of beauty, each object perfectly poised.

Violetta spoke, bringing him back to reality. "You're good be a banker. Old Guthrie was dead set against it but you again maneu. him to bankroll the Petrus Christus. I hear that he might become chairman of the board after they bury Andrew."

Jan sat back, oddly handsome with his long, combed-back hair and glossy face, and he regarded his companion-in-arms a most resourceful counterpart to himself. With her pert features and smothering black hair, Violetta reposed in a black dress on a white sofa, framed against a spotless, textureless white wall, all of which almost formed a frieze. The white sofa and white carpet contrasted ever so slightly with the white wall. He adored white on white. As in a painting, he felt he and his wife were removed from the urgencies, the values, of others.

"Yes, Old Guthrie takes over, we own the Petrus Christus and everything is the same. Unfortunately. I preside over the few gems the museum gains, but just as many are lost to wealthier institutions. We move at the whim of the financiers. They are the power brokers and I feel like an impotent observer, watching longingly as the art parade passes me by. I blame the trustees every time they lose the art objects I covet, because they don't have the financial balls to back me up."

"Of course!" Violetta said. "You are the one who selects the material to be purchased. The museum couldn't manage without your guidance. They need you. Your hands shouldn't be tied."

"Yes, but my hands are tied. Even an art dealer buys what he wants when he wants it, but I can't."

Yet he knew himself better. He was a museum man through and through, devising schemes and selling them, taking orders and executing them. He didn't crave personal risks involving his own money, while art dealers plunge into financial speculation, a pursuit not for him. In the eyes of his professional peers his career would soon peak, unless he could sufficiently free himself to initiate the major moves, moves that would transform the museum into a leader in its field.

"But there's a new twist," he emphatically pronounced. "Something irregular has arisen, a wrinkle to consider, a small deviation that might provide an opportunity for us. The trustees have changed the bylaws. As of now there is no acquisition board."

"I see," she nodded slowly. "Maybe it's for the best. Why do you need the board? Those cumbersome old farts don't know anything about art. They simply get in your way. Here's our chance at last. Take it."

"Yes, my dearest heart, as usual, you're right. We agree on this as we do on everything else. You know I would be doing the museum a favor if I traded all the junk donated to us that clutters the storage rooms. Trading from the museum's collection is tricky business. We must be careful—no slip-ups."

"With caution," she smiled. "Definitely carry on but continue with great caution. Nothing will stop you."

The next day Old Guthrie sat with Jan in the museum cafeteria. "Do you think we should continue the acquisition board? Should we bother with it?"

Jan pleasantly tolerated the amiable old fool because he was docile, and Guthrie often took Jan's ideas for his own. But this time Jan chose to look offended and exclaimed, "What am I doing as your director? If you have no confidence in me, I can always remove myself."

"No!" Guthrie blurted. "No, don't say that. You know we believe in you. Implicitly! What with your taste and the fact that you have practically single-handedly created the museum? No, don't you mind. Besides, board members grumble about convening for meetings every time you propose an acquisition at some goddamn uncomfortable hour. Don't you mind. We'll let them cool their heels for a while. They can take a break. Later on we'll start again."

"Whenever," Jan shrugged. "I think this could be our best year with you at the helm."

It occurred quite casually. Old Guthrie unwittingly gave his consent for Jan to operate alone; he now had the necessary authority. He was no longer the trustees' minion. Proceed with caution; his wife had preached caution. Ostensibly, nothing must change on the surface. He would receive no benefits, would live as he had. No extra money, although that never attracted him. Money existed solely to purchase art, not necessarily the most expensive, ostentatious works, but those chosen aesthetically by a trained eye. He laughed when, surprisingly, the trustees gave him a raise. A vote-of-confidence raise for his museum leadership. A raise to do what he now most desired. Perfection! A little Shakespearean ego factor exists here, he chided himself, as he thought about fate. Surely he was tickling it, or better, sweetly stroking it.

No, he would never own the big ticket numbers, the Rembrandt, Goya, Vermeer, Velasquez. But Jan had always desired to engineer the purchase of a superb Courbet for the museum. He spotted a beauty on the open market in Brussels. On the heels of financing the Petrus Christus the museum could ill afford to purchase a superlative Courbet. He had drained the trustees' finances; they needed time to recuperate. How could he accomplish this delicate feat?

Whenever Jan viewed the Ruisdael landscape the museum was given by Andrew's great uncle forty years earlier, he felt uneasy. First, it was visually weak. Second, it could be a fake, but it seemed to pass all the tests, so the experts validated it. Third, in spite of its large size, which would normally help the piece to realize a considerable price, the painting misfired. It seemed not quite finished, or rather it was executed in the tradition of the Dutch-Flemish school of landscape painting without painstaking care. But it could be hyped. It looked grand and impressive. There were no restrictions on selling the piece. Andrew's great uncle had attached no stipulations.

Through agents he let it out that the museum was disposing of its esteemed marvels, and simultaneously he began negotiating for the Courbet. If he could garner it, he would improve the museum's holdings, as well as fiercely revel in his own prowess. It turned out that the canvas was for sale in name only. The owners became skittish about parting with it and removed it from the market. Undaunted, Jan obtained the best legal advice for them about tax advantages that would ease the pain of releasing their trophy. His ploy worked. He could now almost taste the painting's succulent, plump, effulgent, richly red apples lying on an endless table.

Meanwhile, the Ruisdael made its debut among the most respectable European art dealers. Jan adroitly lowered the inflated price and had a strike; a Dutch collector bought it. The Courbet cost a little more than he received for the landscape, but Jan covered his deficit by withdrawing funds from an open account available to him. All in all, a splendid trade, one that didn't hurt a bit. He was glad to see the Ruisdael go; he had always been suspicious of it. Besides, he got to enjoy the Courbet just as if he was a collector.

Soon after, but not too soon for propriety's sake, he was back on course. A magnificent Northwest Coast Indian house screen surfaced from a Tlingit tribe in Alaska. A rare and fabulous find and American, too, circa 1800, one of the few remaining epic-size totemic carvings, the size of an Egyptian tableaux. He liked to think American at times. It was too easy, too stylish and certainly too safe to always go with European, flat-art, over-priced paintings. But the price was staggering. The assembled screen had been taken from its location in an Indian village and stored in Oregon for ten years, while a law suit was pending to establish its legal ownership. The moment the wondrous screen was free and clear Jan pushed forward. But one obstacle held him back. Although legally cleared, the tribal family owners had not yet decided to part with their cherished ancestral screen. A trip to the hinterland was in order.

In Angoon, on the Island of Annette near Sitka, Jan found waterways flecked with islands, peninsulas, inlets, whales and brown bears. The family lived in what resembled a Victorian Midwestern farm house, surrounded by tall trees. Two stories made of cedar and fir with shingle roof and siding sheltered an aged Indian couple, who anticipated his arrival.

Judging from the period clothes they wore, Jan surmised that they possessed the early thirties mentality of Sears and J. C. Penney catalogues. He searched them for any telltale signs of what to expect when he bargained with them. They seemed distant, out of touch with the clanging, crashing world. But these isolated spirits sweetly told him that they wanted four million dollars for their prize. To illustrate their point they held up four out-spaced fingers. Jan sighed, grunted and signed a general outline of the agreement, and then he left.

To gain the screen he traded a magnificent ancient Greek vase. This time it pained him. He admitted that the vase screamed greatness, and the trade offended his sensibility. There was no steal here. He gave equally, treasure for treasure. Nonetheless, he justified the exchange. The museum owned three superior Greek vases, while it did not own a Northwest Coast house screen, nor was it likely to.

So it went and smoothly. He masterfully bartered. Sometimes he gained no particular edge in his trades. In the competitive market he could not always be expected to come out a winner. He gave and received good value. Occasionally he fretted about offering too much and his adversary (or in polite terms, his associate) getting the better of him. He felt this when he noticed that he had thinned out an especially strong collection of early Japanese earthenwares.

One boundary he never crossed. He was meticulous about not accepting any considerations, rewards, gratuities or gifts. He just played benign dealer and he excelled at it. Along with taking exciting trips to track down his art quarry, Jan met the foremost art merchants in the world. He was accorded respect as a knowledgeable art dealer who carried along with him the vast resources of his museum. He had art muscle.

To his immense satisfaction Jan Vandergrift had unrestricted freedom. No one knew what he was adding to the museum or seemed to care. No one bothered. He was sometimes offered gifts, which he always refused, the only exception being once in Northern India when he decided it was permissible to accept the present of a fake Gandhara statue of Buddha. It was such an excellent copy he was almost convinced it was real. However, he doubted if the Buddha was fifty years old and he quietly accepted the gift.

◆

There came a day when Old Guthrie tentatively presented to the trustees the issue of reestablishing an acquisition board. After a respite of two years of inaction, the board answered affirmatively. It had overcome its previous inertia.

The board met. Jan presided. Business continued as usual, except that the power to use funds or formulate trades was denied him. No longer able to carry on his personal barter system, Jan was somewhat relieved. He was drowning in his own intrigues. He had performed his part as far as he could; the museum profited, while he hadn't profited one cent.

But his firmament began to crack beneath him. A young lawyer joined the board and asked to inspect the museum's inventory records. Several department heads were delegated to assist him. The man was most proficient. Inquiries were made. The lawyer, with a barrister-sounding name of Samuel Quick, of the firm Quick, Quick and Hammer, held a private meeting with Jan and asked a few questions. Some museum art objects were missing and unaccounted for. Did Jan know of their whereabouts? Jan did. He showed the young man his records involving the trades. He in turn asked to study them and Jan consented. In this most orderly procedure all was accounted for.

No, not quite all. The museum added an accountant to the staff whose name Jan could never quite catch, but he associated it with a Mr. Bleak or Creep. The fellow was obviously directed to research Jan's previous transactions. Jan was not told what his findings revealed. Not only that, he seemed to be partially shut out of official trustee business. He was now performing basic curatorial duties, which with some exaggeration he felt were akin to dusting objects, straightening paintings and ordering new light fixtures. What perhaps bothered him most was that he and his dearest wife were not invited by Old Guthrie to attend a lavish formal dinner party, heretofore a required social outing at the mansion. Without ever being a member of a storm watch group, Jan knew a storm was impending.

The new Dickensian accountant handed Jan the summons that requested him to attend a special trustees meeting to be held at Regal Hall the next afternoon at 4:00 P.M.

That night Jan told Violetta about the forthcoming trustees' meeting. She sat nestled against a huge black pillow on the white sofa. Since the foreboding events had begun, the room seemed to take on a disjointed quality that mirrored their predicament.

"The whole group hasn't met in the Regal Hall since President Gerald Ford paid the trustees an honorable visit," he declared.

"We are honorable, too, damn it!" exploded Violetta. "Everything's not simply black and white. Not at all. All the museum people here from the East Coast agree that, while you were in charge, the most brilliant art pieces passed into the museum galleries, that you greatly augmented the collection."

"And yet . . . ." he began.

"No, not at all." She refused to hear him. "You should be praised instead of cast down. You will be roundly congratulated for your performance."

"And yet . . . ." he repeated.

Their eyes met.

"Yes," she murmured, "I know. We are in deep trouble. But did we go too far? I don't think so. We were careful. You had the authority to make every acquisition for the museum."

"Yes, we have a good defense. But my art deals extended far past the boundary of the caution that you warned me about. Yet with luck and certainly some tenacity, maybe we can manage to just squeeze through these dangerous straits. Perhaps."

When Jan entered through the heavy, bolt-riveted wooden doors, he did so with stodgy, conservative steps, not with his former vigor. He moved into a room in which a large, extraordinary Shaker table was ringed by members of the board of trustees dressed in dark suits. It amused him that he had snagged the table for the museum. A matched set of bland English prints of hunting scenes completely covered the walls. Before him, in the stale and static landscape of muddled men, the opulent chandelier above was the only thing alive.

Not a trustee was missing. Jan mused that he alone must necessitate the occasion for this reunion of common souls. He was beckoned to take a solitary seat at the end of the table, and not the usual one next to Old Guthrie. His long descent into his seat allowed his eyes to make a circular pan over the noble faces of each exemplar of stability and solvency.

Old Guthrie glanced hesitantly at the members and stated softly, "Now we may begin." He turned his head around the group to gather in their collective strength, and then he addressed Jan uneasily. "You are here to explain yourself."

Jan bristled. These people who were his judges knew nothing about art, cared nothing about art. But he had to resist a measure of compassion for awkward Old Guthrie who was brought into this mock inquisition against his will.

The nameless accountant came to the point. "The museum is losing many of its finest art works. No one on the board had the slightest inkling of their disappearance until our recent discovery of your operations. Only you possessed the power to consummate art purchases. No one was consulted, no one informed. You single-handedly disposed of items that were not yours to get rid of," and the man threw out his hands as a gesture indicating wanton discard of material. "This institution serves in the same capacity as a trust, wherein the museum's director is required to keep the organization's collection in a trust mandated to preserve its art assets for future generations to enjoy. You have not been given permission to squander these priceless and irreplaceable heirlooms for your personal gratification. Who gave you such a right?"

Jan knew his next answer and the next one after that. He had safe passage.

"I was the only one responsible for acquisitions. No one was there to help me. I did the best I could. With the museum constantly in debt, the only way to acquire great art was for me to conduct trades in the museum's favor, to its advantage. Otherwise, there is no feasible method for a major museum to continue to dynamically grow and compete with its rivals."

The lawyer Quick reminded Jan that until relatively recently there was an operating acquisition policy. Why didn't he reconvene the acquisition board when he felt compelled to add new material?

"Clearly," responded Jan, "the fact is that there was no board; the board simply did not exist. But more to the point, who is better qualified to render artistic judgments and decisions than the director? Who?"

Immediately Quick countered, "That is no way to run a museum. It should not run on mere whim. You have no experience as an art dealer. None at all. You trade a masterpiece for a masterpiece. We add an irreplaceable piece and lose another. Who wins? Why should we lose any? Why should the museum gamble away its heritage just to play games? If we cannot afford an object, then we can wait until we can buy it. But to frivolously drain away-no, dissipate-our collective art legacy is a sin, a crime!"

Jan diagnosed that the tribunal would finally wind down to the key question of legality, and on that issue he was impervious to its attack. He had prepared his case well. But he must strongly represent his position.

"There is no decent museum without its art, especially significant art; otherwise, it's a shell. Obtaining art is the museum's main business, my business. You understand?" Then he calmed himself. "Even so, I have committed no crime. Everything I have accomplished has been achieved legally."

The accountant asked, "Have you received money or remuneration in any kind from your trading activities?"

"No, absolutely not, none at all," Jan replied.

Jan calculated that he needed no more answers. He did not have any, either.

But surprisingly Old Guthrie took over. "Except for one slip, one mistake you made."

Jan appraised the New Guthrie.

"Mr. Quick informs me that he found a memorandum in your desk stating that you were given a stone figure of a Buddha-you call it a Gandhara sculpture-which you display in your office. A gift, shall we describe it, from an East Indian collector you have been dealing with. Yes, a gift."

"That piece is a fake. It is worthless. That is why I accepted it, because it has no value. I have received no financial rewards whatsoever," Jan averred.

"Not quite so," the accountant parried. "You're not off the hook, not quite. We had the sculpture in question professionally examined. Not to dispute your expertise, Mister Director, but we found that under a recently applied layer of a thick, stubborn coating, very hard to remove, lies a classic Gandhara figure of great age and value. Mind you, of museum quality. Mind you, we are talking a quarter of a million dollars."

Jan replayed the scene when he had obtained the stone sculpture. Whose mistake? Could the dealer have made such an error as to give him a real jewel? Impossible!

"There has been a mistake," Jan insisted. "You can contact the owner of the piece yourself. He will tell you it is not authentic."

"I assure you we will," Guthrie retorted, "and I might as well inform you that we are investigating how you raided the museum's open account. But, needless to say, I think it is common knowledge that, as of this meeting, your services with this institution are terminated. Our lawyer will contact you."

Guthrie's words-needless to say-echoed within him as the trustees left the room. Needless to say-dammit he knew art, had gorged on art. Its sumptuous feast he had tasted excruciatingly, yes, tasted endlessly.

Jan looked down the empty conference table. White scratch pads like place mats were in front of each trustee's chair. He had filled similar museum rooms with his collection of art. Better the Courbet still life, the Northwest Coast screen and the whole heavenly host of wonders he had amassed than the motley group who had just vacated the dozen chairs around the superb pine table. Without regret he had fulfilled his vision.

A fierce radiance kindled his eyes.

IN LOVE'S DOMINION

LOREN, LOREN ENSOR, WAS HARDLY A good friend of mine. One day we met by chance at an art cinema theater and decided to watch a weak and pretentious French film together. Few people knew Loren; he rarely extended himself in conversation. My group of oddball college friends credited him with being wealthy because he wore fine tweed sport coats with shirts and ties. On occasion the gleam of a cashmere sweater pinned with an Adlai Stevenson election campaign button would catch the eye. His thin red hair and considerable measure of Old World charm led us to believe he was somewhat older than we were and especially more experienced.

But there is little point in continuing on about Loren. He was simply the catalyst for my story-really an awful story that I am not proud of.

Anyway, the film unraveled to its sorry end and as we left the place, I mentioned that he had brought no woman with him. What made Loren singular to me was his record of achievements with women and the fact that one was always wedged inside his arm whenever I saw him at a classical concert or an art gallery. I always ambled around by myself or with a boring chum.

"Women have their place," he shrugged. "I like having one every other day, but there must be some spaces in between or I tire of them."

I remarked that I was tired of being without them. He laughed and told me about this girl that he no longer went out with whom I might like.

"She's a poet," he added, "a serious working poet. I looked over her poems with her. She works at a few jobs she doesn't like in order to be able to write poetry."

"There is a serious side to me," I said. "Believe it or not, I also write poetry. I'm really involved."

"Then you two might make a good match," he explained. "But I tell you, she is a bit strange. She's shapely and you can and will go all the way with her-yes, she is certainly physical enough," and he shook his head, "but that's her problem. She tries to resist, knowing she shouldn't become so easily aroused, and the struggle she goes through just tears her up. You have to be careful. She wants to be considered a poet-be seen as a poet, not as an easy woman."

"I am a poet," I asserted, "and I can relate to her as a poet. How come you stopped seeing her?"

"She's not for everyone. Apparently she was sexually molested as a young girl and got used to it. She's all mixed up about being cared for and loved and that sort of thing. I guess I didn't give her what she wanted, so we ended the relationship."

"Thanks for the word. I'll see what I can do. What is her name?"

"Stacey Childress. You might have seen me with her. I'll give you her telephone number."

That was all. Loren is no longer important or necessary to this tale. What happened is no fault of his.

I called Stacey Childress and distorted Loren's escorting her around to mean that I had seen her with my friend at a concert. Of course I told her I wrote poetry like she did, and that I, in general, was a poet, according to my good friend Loren. I suggested maybe we could meet somewhere and discuss poetry. Naturally.

She hesitated. "Bring my poetry with me? I don't know you. But, of course, if you want to know me, I will have to bring my poems. They are my friends."

We decided that since she owned no car, a friend of hers would drive her to my apartment in the middle of Los Angeles, not far from where she lived. We were to meet in three days. For the occasion I borrowed a yellow cashmere sweater from Loren to impress her and to bring me the same luck he had possessed. I bought a bottle of inexpensive wine from some remote country I've forgotten the name of and placed it on the coffee table.

During the interval I retrieved two buried notebooks of poetry from inside the lid of the piano bench in which sheets of music were stored. I glanced at them guardedly. They were aged, if not quite old, slightly stale; no effervescence left. I skimmed some lines.

> I'll love you if you'll love me,
> I must have this guarantee to love;
> Then I'll love your love for me.

What kind of love is this? Ego love. No good love. Stunted poem. I listlessly turned pages and poems slid by like dead weights. I figured my day as a poet was undetermined. Not stillborn or unborn but eternally incubated. What would Stacey think? Not much.

Stacey's ride delivered her an hour late. It didn't matter because it was still early enough in the evening for us to carry out my scenario. I looked her over: big-boned with chocolate brown eyes and hair, a large-framed young woman bestowed with generous proportions. She clutched to her side a small black, leather-bound book and placed it ceremoniously on the coffee table.

"There it is," she quietly announced, "the good book," and this seemed to validate her reason for being here. She took off a coarse cotton coat, flicked back her thick, neck-length hair and sat down. She had a certain urgency about her that permeated the room. She glanced around but didn't respond to my special modern Scandinavian stick furniture. She could be sitting anywhere at anytime but not specifically in my room with me.

"Would you like a bottle of wine-red?" I asked.

"No, I don't drink."

"You must not come from Los Angeles because no one is born here, and you don't look like a native." I smiled at my attempt at humor.

"No, but I seem to be here on a long visit."

"Where are you from?"

"I'm not from much of anywhere. I have lived in Wyoming and Idaho and I just wandered here."

While I was getting nowhere with her, I noticed that her dress was similar to what a nurse wore-white, buttoned down in front, setting off her form most pleasantly. I detected tantalizing swells where, between them, the buttons paraded up and down.

I switched subjects. "Your poetry-what about your work? How long have you been writing?"

Stacey smiled and her whole body began to relax. "When I was quite young I felt a need within me to write poetry. I didn't have any idea who I was; I couldn't explain myself to myself or to others. I simply could not cope, so I wrote poems. A lot of verse. I had to. I could personalize myself through poetry. Some of my poems still remain young and so I continue to improve them. They are all like one long poem."

"Sounds like therapy."

The concept amused her. "Therapy! Yes, little pieces of therapy. Poems work that way. Don't you become lost when you are not writing verse? You lose all direction, like an ant without its antennae."

"I am always in a bog and so I never go anywhere. I just know the geography of my bog. Me and my bog."

"That's terrible," she exclaimed and reached out and almost touched me out of pity. "Your irony is amusing. But how can you accept yourself in that state of mind?"

"I am not always serious," I slightly revealed myself. "I like to play.

But, yes, I am quite accustomed to not doing much-resigned to muddle through the days, though I can't say I'm happy about it. I am as unmoored as the lost ant you described. But tell me, what has poetry actually done for you? Did it help you at home when you were young?"

"Oh, you will never know! I had no home. Or I had three homes. Each was a horror. Every time I packed my possessions to go from one house to another I would have rather died than return. Finally the houses ran out on me; there was no place for me to go."

"You mean, you're an orphan?" I asked, puzzled.

"Yes," she said reluctantly. "When there were no more houses, I took a bus to here."

She looked so forlorn, so mired in hopelessness, so vulnerable that I instinctively reached out and enfolded her in my arms. As I absorbed her body into mine, I felt genuinely sympathetic and for a moment wanted to protect her, but then my desire to have a woman engulfed me and I embraced her fiercely.

She stiffened, began to withdraw, retreat. Not willing to release her, I clutched her tightly and began to intone in her ear the earlier love verse of mine I had discovered, now purposely altered to ensnare her.

> I'll love you, you'll love me;
> We shall have this guarantee
> To create our own reality.

Softening, she clung to me. Her breathing quickened. She murmured, "I like poets-being a poet. You are one, even if you deny it. You can't help being poetic."

I licked my assent on her neck just underneath her hair and into her ear. She moved abruptly away and I tried to ease her back. My fingers grabbed and accidentally (I like to think accidentally) tore open some of the buttons of her dress. To my surprise I gaped at her unforgettable breasts barely tucked into a tattered, yellowed brassiere. For an instant I thought of protecting her by carefully placing her breasts back into their shelters. Before she could react, I made my move toward her, but she quickly fell forward on the sofa to cover herself. I was able to pull her onto her back, and with my weight holding her down, I began to disrobe her. My fingers became entangled in opening the maddening buttons on her dress, guardians of her vanished chastity. Her head turned from side to side.

She pleaded: "Please don't go any further. I shouldn't do this. I shouldn't." A slight rasping sound escaped her lips.

I tried to unclasp the hooks of her brassiere but they seemed to be welded. I noticed that her features were distorted; her eyes went upward and the cords on her neck tightened and enlarged.

"All right," I said, as I dropped my hand. "I don't understand-don't want to understand. You can't expect me to stop. Not now. I want you. Anyway, you want the same thing."

"Wait! Let me explain. Don't do anything," and she shoved her hands forward as a shield. "If you only knew. I had to raise myself. You don't know anything about me. I'm lost. If you like me-maybe you do-or if you have any regard for me just as a person-then let me go. I feel like I am splitting apart. You're a poet; please understand. I could like you. Help me!"

Not her kind of poet I thought; I'm a poet in action. There was no way I could stop. It was too late. Fumbling, I pulled down her panties.

In an instant she changed into a fury. She wriggled frantically and turned on me: her nails cut me, her feet bunched and kicked me with the power of a mule. I hurt. I relaxed my grip on her. Then rapidly, with amazingly charged energy, she severed herself from me by thrusting a knee into my stomach and pulled herself away. She slid off the sofa, swept up her dress and in a blur of motion slipped out of the apartment, leaving the door open.

I counted every second of her exit. I could have stopped her, but my one decent move was to make no move at all. I could have had her, but I couldn't sufficiently concentrate on subduing her. She bothered me. But she pleased me. What next? I very calmly-too calmly because I was unnerved-arose and shut the door. She had undoubtedly dressed herself by now. However, she forgot her heavy, nondescript oxfords and her coat. Furthermore, I had promised to drive her home. She had to walk now but it wasn't far. She could manage.

But then I saw it. Of course it still would be there, a testimony to my screw up, or perhaps a shrine to the Sacred Heart-her heart. There was the black leather book of poetry. I nodded at it. She had no time to retrieve it before she made her escape. Escape was the proper word, escape from me. And yet she left a vital part of herself behind. I decided to ignore it; it was hers, not mine. Although Loren had told me about Stacey's aberrational sexual behavior, maybe I would have fared better if I hadn't known and had treated her differently. Maybe if I went to bed now and tried to sleep, I could blot out the mess I had created. So I retired.

For two days I left the book inviolate on the table. Surely Stacey would return, was bound to retrieve her poems, her "friends," as she called them. Then I would talk to her. Meanwhile, I didn't want to further aggravate her. I could try to explain myself but I considered it a waste of time. I probably disgusted her and rightly so, I suppose. Although I owned an important part of her, I owed her no obligation. It was she who abruptly vacated my abode. Even if I forced myself to concede that I was the attacker and she the victim, I resented her evading my conquest. I still could deliver her poems to her, exert the supreme gesture, but I simply could not do it, would not do it. She would be back. Through her poetry I had some control over her actions. Anyway, missing her poems would hurt her. I partially relished the situation.

Another day gone. No Stacey. It was like her to be emotionally unpredictable. She had a natural disposition of goodness, a good soul, but her life was roughly hewn. In her wake I would play a game with her: I would appoint the day to read her poems, and when I finished, I would burn them. A barbaric act but nevertheless the terms of my game. But before that ceremony would be enacted, Stacey would materialize; I had no doubt of it.

The day of unveiling arrived. I presided over the launching of the short, thin volume. I sniffed at it, inspected the grainy leather cover, and violating its sanctity I opened it. I focused on a poem written with clear printed letters strongly embedded on the paper. Printed letters meant exacting labor. Her firm, sure hand dominated the paper.

> I shall love you lightly
> Wrapped in downy cloth,
> Through the days and nightly
> Softer than a moth,
> With a love so sprightly
> Flung of ocean froth,
> Finely sprayed and lightly
> You shall be my troth.
> I shall love you brightly.

Definitely a love poem, I chuckled. What else? Overstated, emphatic love. Romantic gush. But she means it; she just simply loves. I riffled through more poems filled with love tracts and declarations. I latched on to one.

> When I loved you more
> in the throes of that
> fixed fascination I
> would have written love words
> on chairs and cigarettes
> and placed them in
> Egypt's tomb for future
> passersby to find them.
> They were good verses;
> now they lie in knots
> of tattered sound.
> I envy my self's past sojourn
> into the citadel of love.

Did she work through love's exaltation? Now she was becoming more mortal and human, accepting even tarnished love. Diminished love that ended. Yes, she was definitely appealing to me. Then I came across a prose piece at the end of Stacey's book, a block of straight prose.

There was a girl who was loved completely by a boy. Not piece by piece, like an idea starting a smile or the shoulder gliding into the neck. For him the idea, smile, shoulder, neck, all shot out and became a lovely girl. The boy just gathered her shimmers and loved. The girl loved, too, and they dwelled together in peace.

There came a day when the boy loved the girl even more. He loved the girl through the world and the world through the girl. The girl said to him, "I love you most of all, except for God!" Now the girl met a stranger and he said, "I am God," and she answered, "I love you, my God." Then the girl went to the boy to introduce him to God. But the boy did not see God and only gazed at the girl. The girl flushed angrily, "You are blind and foolish. You are missing God," and she walked away with God. The boy saddened and wanted to call to her that she was alone, all alone. He watched the others who came around her and they were mistakenly talking to God. The boy stood by himself and looked at the girl and loved.

"Thank God, the end!" I exulted. The curtain came down on the triumphant last act in love's dominion. Now we have distilled love. Only sublime love will do here. Is there enough love to go around? Not for her. With uneasy feelings I completed the book and Stacey still had not appeared. I would wait a week before I began my last rites for her poems.

I busied myself by calling friends and talking incessantly on the telephone. I thought of talking to Loren but I desisted. I marveled that I was only a telephone call away from Stacey. Just a little patch of land traversed by talking wires separated us. But the two of us were fixed points of reference; we could not move. Within our respective houses we did nothing. To me the whole event assumed the proposition of an ill-fated love story. I fussed and fumed intermittently. Even if I waited days longer or to the end of the next week it would make no difference. She would not reclaim her poetry and her shoes and coat. They were dead property. Not hers anymore. She had repudiated me by outlasting me, by certainly maintaining the last word of strength and endurance. She won even though I had her trophies. But now they were my booty-those personal poems that I could hardly equal. Maybe I could, if

I tried to be a real poet.

I chose a day to execute the dark deed I felt compelled to perform. I considered this ritual an original poetic gesture. An act of power. After all, I gave her enough time to comply. In the morning, around 10:30, I left my apartment and sauntered back to where four incinerators stood in a row. Smoke belched from the third one. No one saw me. Nearly all of the occupants of the apartments were at work.

Carrying the book in one hand, I stopped uncertainly and shifted it to the other hand. It was weightless. I stood poised. Then I strode to the burning incinerator, pulled open the lid and thrust the black book inside. I watched for a second as the pages began to recoil in the flames and wad up together. I closed the lid, stepped back, regarded the smoke and retraced my steps. I had just burned a lot of love.

Enough of love. I was relieved of it. I decided that I was not entirely unhappy. I wondered how I was going to dispose of Stacey's shoes and coat. And what about Loren–did he know about me and Stacey? More than ever I had to concede that Loren had sensitive taste.

But it was dismally true: I had no valid explanation for my act.

THE LAMB AND THE WOLF

THE BOY WAS PRIVILEGED OF SORTS. HE came from a middle class Los Angeles family, with an insurance broker father and a mother at home who presided over a maid the family could hardly afford. Sometimes his mother was paid to decorate her friends' houses with curtains, sofas, chairs and carpets, all homogenized into utter blandness, one house indistinguishable from another. His father, incrementally paying a long standing debt incurred during the Depression, had difficulty making ends meet, which caused the mother to worry. However, in an unusual move his parents managed to give the boy a set of the *World Book Encyclopedia*. The gift surprised and delighted Ian, since his father wanted him to be a well-rounded, sports-minded boy (as he had been), not one particularly filled with encyclopedic knowledge. His parents–she, tall, lanky, sharp-edged and he, short, roundish, jolly, even-tempered–appreciated the reaction of their twelve year-old son.

But Ian didn't read, he just looked at pictures. Obsessed with wild animals from all over the world, he collected hundreds of picture books on the subject. Nothing else interested him. His fascination with the animal pictures precluded all reading. Mr. Roper finally convinced his son that if he wanted to learn more about all these animals, he would have to learn to read. Ian bought this thesis. "The closer I can get to tigers, my favorite, and all the others, the better," he smiled, and he began to read.

Volumes of the *World Book Encyclopedia* were scattered around the house with their pages lying open according to the animals featured, Volume T for the Tasmanian Wolf or Volume O for the Ounce, which he also knew as the snow leopard. Soon his reputation as an expert on wild animals spread. Through friends of his parents he attracted the attention of Martin and Osa Johnson, and Frank Buck, who directed wildlife documentary films in Africa and Asia. As the beguiling, freckled, hazel-eyed and tawny-haired child wizard of the animal kingdom, he was offered an opportunity to join them on their film safaris. His father said, by all means, yes; his mother said no, because Ian had a habit of flunking his mathematics classes at the public school. His mother won out.

Yes, he disliked math. Ian couldn't see any relationship between algebra and an okapi or a wombat. "Math sucks!" he declared. In order for him to graduate, his father performed a vital ritual every time the school term ended. He presented the teacher, Mrs. Frakes, with a box of See's candy in exchange for a passing grade. Ian calculated that it cost his father a considerable effort to persuade the good woman to think kindly of him, mathematically speaking.

As a general practice, Mr. Roper liked to discuss with his son the progress Ian was making. "I am happy about you. You're coming along nicely. You're no longer just interested in wild animals and have branched out. Good. And you're reading lots of books."

Ian remarked, "It's no longer a chore. I like to read now, Dad. You've really helped me."

There were other items on the father's agenda that he wanted to introduce to his son, but first he intended to put to rest the matter of his deficiency in math. "I still don't think you've done as well with mathematics as you might have," he laughed. "Your teacher says you and math can't get along together. By the way, I'm changing my brand of candy. I think Mrs. Frakes is tiring of See's.

"Furthermore, when I was a boy, I was taught that a gentleman acquired skills playing sports, which I did. This helped me develop some degree of physical coordination. It would be good for you, too. I'm looking for a place where you can be trained.

"I've been planning ahead to when you will be graduating from high school and going to a university. When you're there, I hope you take some business courses to prepare for the future. You'll meet people, make friends, study economics, everything in good order, and you'll learn how to handle yourself on all occasions. Maybe, at one point, after you've seen a bit of the world, you'll want to join my insurance business. That shouldn't concern you now, though. You'll have plenty of time to grow up."

"I feel fine, Pops, thanks to you," Ian replied. "You've done a lot for me."

Ian Roper, at the age of twelve, was enrolled in a special boy's club, where he was to be fashioned manly and molded into an athlete. Three times a week after school his mother would take him to what was deemed to be the "blue-blooded institution," and after two hours of his serious application, pick him up and return him home. At the "institution" there was a swimming pool, gymnasium and a tennis court in the center of an asphalt field where track meets were held. Although he derived greater pleasure from his encyclopedia, Ian rather enjoyed engaging in sports, something he was performing with a measure of excellence. Because he liked his Dad enormously, and his Dad thought it was to his benefit to compete successfully in organized sports, Ian went along with his Dad's plans.

Ian was particularly adept in the fifty-yard dash. He was continually told by his eager schoolmates that certain students said they could beat him in a race, and in between classes he would set up meetings with each challenger and race him. He won every contest.

The sports club turned out to be first-rate, much to Ian's satisfaction. He soon blended in smoothly with his companions, and since he was well-coordinated he had no trouble keeping up with the various activities. In track he was still one of the best sprinters.

As a swimmer he was tops. When Ian was introduced to water polo, he swam so fast he was usually first in retrieving the ball. Once in a frantic melee of players who were racing for the ball, he jumped up to spear it, missed, and as he came down, accidentally whacked the ear of Mr. Lockwood, the swimming instructor. The coach momentarily shook his head and tilted it sideways but continued to referee. Intermittently, he would briefly stop and tap the base of his ear and then stroke it with the palm of his hand. Finally, when the game ended, he called the players to gather around him. He told them that someone had crashed into him and banged his ear during the free play and he couldn't hear out of his right ear. It wasn't working and he didn't know if it ever would. He asked if anyone had seen who had done the deed, with the understanding that it was a mistake. The boys looked around at each other and Ian could tell that no one knew. He remained silent. Poor Mr. Lockwood shrugged his shoulders and climbed out of the pool. Ian was displeased with himself, particularly so because his swimming instructor never shook his deafness. Ian never mentioned the incident to his father. He wouldn't have considered it progress.

The manly art of self-defense was emphasized. Instruction in boxing was offered and every member had to fight at least one time. A boxing ring was installed in the middle of the gymnasium, and according to age, weight and experience, each person was assigned to a class of boxers. Ian was placed in the lightweight division. Although he was not keen on it, he was remarkably suited to prize fighting. His footwork of weaving in and out, ducking, crouching, quickly advancing and retreating with legs springy and yet taut, caught the eye of the boxing coach, who gave Ian special pointers. Ian's hands were lightning fast, especially his left jab directed straight and hard at his adversary with the blurred thrust of a venomous reptile and then just as speedily withdrawn to cover his body and face. His boxing partners fared poorly for Ian couldn't be hit, and if one stray blow managed to find its way toward his head, his guarded right hand would brush it off. Meanwhile, his left hand, ever flitting, poking, prowling, would sting his foe into confusion and despair. What he scarcely conceived happened: he had evolved into a killing machine.

A boxing tournament was scheduled, and the parents and friends of the club and its pupils were invited. Naturally Ian's parents received an invitation, an embossed card declaring the event, much like the heralding of a medieval jousting affair. The father was tickled; he had not yet seen his boy perform. The mother thought that sitting among a throng of sophomoric simpletons was out of the question and she planned to stay away. Ian observed that his father was pleased. He talked about a purpose being accomplished–the emergence of his son.

Over a hundred spectators, many old friends and alumni, came to view the junior gladiators. Ian located his short and stout father sitting next to and conversing with the slender and towering Mr. Blumberg, who was the father of Emmanuel Blumberg, a friend and fellow student. Tall, gangly, redheaded and freckled, Emmanuel was a confirmed scholar who didn't know why he was there and felt he had no connection with this hopeless enterprise. He had long ceased to pay any attention to his father's wish for him to round out his intellectually-steeped education. He was destined to be a physicist and matriculate at the California Institute of Technology near Los Angeles. Comfortable in a laboratory, he could not fathom a boxing ring.

Mr. Roper wore his work suit and tie, as did Mr. Blumberg, and the two of them were enjoying each other. Mr. Arrow, the boxing coach, stepped to a microphone and announced that every combatant would fight three opponents, each for three rounds. Both Ian and Emmanuel were designated as lightweights.

For his first fight Ian was given an awkward young man, slow and pudgy, who stood in the middle of the ring. With minimum effort he kept rotating, trying to face Ian. Ian was perpetually encircling the boy, the centerpiece of his focus, darting his left hand out and pelting him with searing jabs, which caused red welts on his arms and body and a few on his face. The victim turned in a tight circle while Ian, displaying his dexterous footwork, whizzed by his lumbering adversary. Toward the end, Ian's human target turned pink over his entire body, as if he was consumed by fever. Mr. Roper simply beamed when his son was declared the victor and after that he talked more volubly to Mr. Blumberg.

Ian's next fight was against Emmanuel Blumberg. The fathers quieted down and settled seriously into their seats. Ian generated speed and agility, pedaling all over the ring, flicking his left glove into Emmanuel's eyes and digging it into his face and nose, pummeling his mouth and inflicting four blows to every one in return. Not that Emmanuel didn't gamely try to retaliate, but he hated what he was doing. He lunged at Ian, flailing away with long, swinging, looping blows, easily deflected. He closed his eyes, lowered his head, clenched his lips and tried to charge into Ian, who was never there but elsewhere, pecking at his nose and forehead, churning, bobbing.

Through the fuzzy din of the yelling crowd, Ian detected the excited voice of his father, and the increasingly angry voice of Mr. Blumberg. At that moment, Ian was surprised to find Emmanuel's right nostril cut and bleeding. He wondered why he hadn't noticed it before, perhaps because he was prancing around too much. But it was there and he went for it. He poked it, badgered it, slashed at it, teased and bothered it. The nostril's edge was severed and red drops began to fall.

Clearly distinct now from the audience's drone, his father was screaming, "That's it! That's it! Smash him, crush him to a pulp, tear off his nose. You got him. Finish him off before the bell rings."

Rivaling these tirades with equal bombast was Mr. Blumberg's high, piercing disgust. "You are not trying. You're not man enough to be here. Coward! Quitter! I am ashamed to have you as my son."

Out of the corner of his eye Ian could now see his father, normally a mild-mannered man, rabidly shouting, the glands of his throat swollen with fervor. "Kill him, destroy him!"

Attempting to concentrate on the partially severed nostril, Ian charted the course of the blood as it filled up the nose, dark and wet, and washed onto the lips and along the edges of the mouth, lapping over the chin and onto the throat, downward. "Finish him off," his father boomed and boomed again. The words, percolating in Ian's mind, woke him, and he flashed that his comrade, Emmanuel, was probably also praying that Ian would finish him off and get the fight over with.

Disgusted with himself, Ian backed away from his rival and disengaged, avoiding contact, continually backtracking. After a minute the bell rang and Ian was decreed the winner. Taking Ian's hand, the referee threw it into the air to the approving shouts of his father.

Feeling sick, Ian soberly walked to his corner of the ring. A senseless massacre, he was thinking. What is this about, anyway, with crazy fathers acting like beasts. But when the bell rang, interrupting his thoughts, he instinctively jumped to his feet, ready for the next bout.

The challenger, Chad Severance, was a member he didn't know very well. He was a year older, worked out with weights and had rippling shoulder muscles. His torso was stout and solid compared to Ian's lithe build. At the start he waded into Ian with authority, persistently advancing with his feet firmly but guardedly planted on the floor. In contrast to Ian's dancing maneuvers, he steadily glided into his attack. He used his right hand, always cocked, ready, poised like an iron club ready to drop. Ian, wary and nimble as usual, circled his man, springing aside when pressed, using his left jab with a stiletto-flicking effect, dodging to escape Chad's advances. Undeterred, Chad relentlessly pursued Ian, and suddenly Chad leveled a right hand blow to Ian's stomach, knocking the wind out of him. Ian, weaving, felt sick. Every step took too much effort. He reeled back, hurt, shocked by the fury of Chad's punches.

Raising his fists, he peppered Chad with a shower of left jabs. Chad shook off the blows and moved in again, crowding Ian. Ian, dodging, was stepping back when Chad let go with a smashing right hand uppercut to his jaw, disconnecting all the parts of his brain. Stunned, but still on his feet, Ian shook his head to clear it. For the first time he now understood how it felt to be the quarry, to be coldly stalked and eliminated. As Chad advanced Ian cagily avoided him, dancing away, feinting and bouncing, never letting Chad come close to him until the fight ended. Chad was awarded the championship.

On the way home his father was sympathetic. "The way I see it, you're a boxer and he's a slugger. You tried your very best. That's what I like," he spoke assuredly. "You were a good sport. You won two and lost one. In the middle fight you were awesome. It was like placing the lamb and the wolf together. It was a slaughter. I am sorry for Mr. Blumberg and the disgrace he had to face. I certainly hope that it will never happen to me."

Ian was sorry, too. He was sorry for Mr. Blumberg, for his comrade, Emmanuel, for himself and above all for his father, whose words stung. Everything felt wrong. His Dad doted on competition. Ian couldn't shake the bloody face of Emmanuel, and for the first time he saw his father in a new light. No matter how hard he tried to be the wolf, no matter how much he loved his father, in the future, to his father's disgrace, he would inevitably be the lamb.

CHARGED AND COMBUSTIBLE MOVEMENT

ANDY AND I WERE CONTENT. WE COMPLIMENTED each other in our work: he, practical and disciplined, and I, emotional and disorganized. As graduates from a decent cinematography school, we were coproducers and directors of our first film in progress, a documentary on building children's personalities through creative dancing, and we were right on schedule. The children's teacher, a former ballerina, had chosen seven children, ages five to eight, from families who lived in the rural neighborhood to dance on a patch of land we cleared for them. We assembled a small film crew with camera and sound equipment and they had been shooting for days, getting good footage. Our three-week time limit was too short, but we couldn't afford to film longer.

In the early morning of the eleventh day, Andy and I huddled together to evaluate our progress. I said, "I'm worried. We're halfway through filming and don't have much going on. We have the little monsters beginning to dance and showing improvement, receiving lots of instruction, but we need to consider an ending, a grand finale. A visual payoff."

"But Lionel, it isn't like that. We get what we get. We've always understood that this film is a chancy experiment, a gamble. We have to simply rely on the teacher using her special images to teach basic movements and then to develop personal styles. Let's see what the kids come up with."

"I realize all that. But if we don't watch out, this will only be a training film for teachers and we don't want that."

"There's nothing wrong with a film which proves we all have talent that a fine teacher can bring out, especially in children before they're brainwashed in schools. Some might have extraordinary abilities and some more ordinary, but whatever comes out is good."

"It's not that. I'm thinking about the film itself, its structure and style. As it stands now, it's flat." Then the idea came. "Do you know what we need?"

"More time and money?"

"No. We need a miracle—we need a star."

"A Hollywood star?" Andy burst forth. "That's exactly what we can do without. Forget the glamour stuff. We still have time. That girl Jenny is an exceptional dancer. Others will develop. It will all work out."

"I'm waiting," I answered.

He laughed, "You're only just waiting for the great dance of Shiva."

That afternoon, after seven hours of filming, I was walking to the campsite when I noticed a little girl ahead of me, playing hard in a neighborhood backyard. Against this quiet, common background, her stirring of charged and combustible movement excited me. Totally absorbed, she was kicking up a storm, dancing to a Sicilian tarantella on the radio. The girl was very little, not much older than a baby, short to the ground and chubby, with dimples, pudgy cheeks and baby fat. Nevertheless, she had considerable mastery of her body as she flew away on dandelion airy feet slightly touching the ground, tiny soarings up, over and down and bouncing back again. I was amazed, but in a flash she saw me and stopped. She looked at me with a shy curiosity and retreated rapidly into the house.

Elated, I told the teacher about my experience. She said that Spring was her name and she was a gifted five year-old pupil of hers. When she had asked Spring's father if he would allow her to be in the movie, he adamantly said no. He told her that his family planned to take a vacation in a week. Frustrated, I offered to talk to this man myself. The teacher agreed but warned that, as a stern and strict Baptist, he would be hard to budge.

At dusk I arrived at the simply built house, really a better-than-average shack. The wood was weathered but also strangely mottled, like something inflicted with skin disease. It stood in a remote wooded area which the county had donated to encourage people to build homes. I knocked on the door. Spring's father opened it guardedly. I could see Spring and her baby brother behind her. "You, you stay back, you hear!" He treated them like pesky dogs.

He stood before me as an ashen gray bulk, with gray face, shirt and pants, and scrabbly hair, too, a man in his forties but tired, dreary.

"You want something?" he grumbled.

"Yes. By chance I saw Spring dance in a backyard this afternoon and she was excellent, quite excellent. Mrs. Prince, you know, the dance teacher, thought she might like to join her playmates and dance with them in front of the movie camera. Spring would enjoy the experience. You would be proud of her. Will you let her go?"

From within Spring squealed. Instinctively, his head jerked toward the noise. "Mrs. Prince is all right, but my girl's not going to dance for you and your movie camera. She's staying home. You're wasting your time. Go away."

"Won't you reconsider? She is a wonderful dancer."

"I said no!" and he abruptly closed the door.

The class began at nine in the morning and Jenny took command. There were five girls and three boys; the boys developed more slowly. I had an assortment of music to choose from: Bach, Mozart, Stravinsky and ethnic folk music. Willowy and energetic, with long, lustrous brown hair, Jenny was a miniature adult, angular, explosive, quick. I selected an Israeli hora for her to try out. She began to swoop in circles and arcs, pounding, stomping with piston-stabbing rhythms to the driving music, arms slashing the air into fragments.

When the dance ended, I remarked to Andy that at least we were lucky to have Jenny. The other students were progressing well enough but I wasn't satisfied. When the noon lunch break arrived, Jenny singled me out.

"Nobody wants lunch. We want to dance."

"But Jenny, you've been dancing for hours and you'll be dancing until this afternoon under the boiling sun with no shade. Don't you want to rest and eat?"

"No, we like to dance. That's why we came here."

"Don't you ever get tired?"

"No, you dance us now," and she searched my face. "We like to do this best."

"Just dance? Is that the only thing?"

"Yes, dance," the group answered in chorus.

"You kids are getting better and better–really good."

At that moment, Jenny turned around and said, "Hello, Spring." It was then that I realized a miracle had occurred.

"Spring!" I beamed. "Did your father change his mind, did he say yes?"

She shook her head up and down, "I asked him and asked him and today he said yes." Her black bangs, cut slightly off-angle, traipsed off her forehead as she fidgeted before me.

"Spring," I said, "I'll tell you what. You're going to dance to some African music we've never played here before. Just for you. It's special. Nobody's heard it. It has a lot of rhythms. Let's see if you can catch each one of them."

Andy checked on Ed and Austin, the camera and sound men, to see if they were primed for the take. The high sounding, eerie, jabbering music, smothered by drum beats, jerked and pricked its way to the awaiting audience. I nodded for Spring to start. She stood stone-still and listened. She tilted her head to one side and then to the other. Then her body crouched low and went into a sliding, rolling motion. She staggered and lurched around the carpet, her feet stuttering to the music's beat. As she took a little jump, she swung her head in circles with closed eyes in a trance, like she blended in harmony with the secrets of the world. Her whirling head moved to one beat, her body, pitching quickly forward, back and around, responded to another, and her sprawled, shuffling leg action pulsated to a third rhythm. All of time held in a dance. A talent that could enthrall the world. Mesmerized, I wondered if even the camera could capture every fleeting, flying element of this overwhelming and fragile drama. The moment the music ceased, she relaxed her body into a slump. A stunned silence ensued.

"What a dance! Austin," I yelled, "you got a good take?"

"Yeah," and he automatically checked his gear. Then he swiftly turned back to me, "No, oh no! The sound wasn't turned on."

"You didn't turn it on," I thundered, "didn't turn the machine on! You didn't record it?"

"I've never done this before," and he stopped at the sudden appearance of Spring's father.

"Enough of this! What I witnessed is wanton behavior. I saw her petticoat showing under her dress when she danced, if you call this dancing. I don't. I call it acting like a wild animal. That's not the way I taught her to act. There's a lot of sin here. Spring! You're coming with me. Quickly! I'm taking you home," and he turned to go.

As Spring moved past me, I whispered, "Spring, what you do is dance. We need you to dance. You're the star!"

Glancing at Austin, I bristled. Then I turned to the group, trying to control myself. "Class, I'm wrong to do this, but I can't help it. There's no more dancing today. I'm sorry."

A plaintive howl of dissent rose from the children. "What will we do if we don't dance? We don't want to go home." I could hear Jenny's voice, the loudest among the mourners.

I charged off, swinging my arms with Andy tagging behind. "Shit," I fumed. "He didn't move the switch. That's all he had to do. With the tiniest gesture of his fingers flick it on. Just a snap," and I sat down on a tree stump.

Andy said, "Don't you think Austin feels bad enough without you piling it on? And the kids? You owe it to them. They're busting their guts out for you. Sure, it's a horrible mistake. We look like amateurs, not professionals. But never mind. It amounts to a mistake; that's all it is."

"You call it a mistake, I call it a fuck up."

"Why be so dramatic?"

"Because that great dance has been obliterated. It's like it never existed. One of mankind's finest moments-lost."

"That's your romantic point of view," Andy said. "If you want the truth, I think you brought this crisis on yourself. We didn't have to have a star or, especially, bring in someone else from outside. That's not the reason for making the film. You asked for the trouble you got. But now it's a dead issue."

"No, it's not dead. It's a living fiery coal burning in my being."

"Listen," Andy said. "You have a film to finish and that's your first priority, and mine, too. Wise up. Right now we have to prepare for tomorrow."

"I know," and wearily I got up and followed him. Still the weight of knowing I couldn't do anything and had to just endure the loss was impossible to bear.

The next day, with the early sun glowing over them, the now sunburn-toughened child dancers were champing at the bit. "The sun's too slow. Why didn't you push the sun up quicker so we could dance sooner?" Jenny asked. Unexpectedly, I spotted Spring, nestling unobtrusively among her friends. She stood out like a desperately scarce white whooping crane in a field of common gray sandhills.

"I'm happy to see you," I said gratefully.

She said softly, "You said dance."

Our eyes met. "Did your father say yes this time?"

She shook her head. "He didn't."

I knew what that meant; we had no time to lose. "Austin, get ready to record fast, and this time no more screw ups. You, Ed, let's shoot." Everything clicked and we were off and running, hoping for a repeat performance.

The drums and screeching created a raw blur of sound. Spring covered her ears to tone down the din. Then she went to work. She was even better than before. She now realized she had dance power, and although the music didn't quite excite her as before, she executed her steps more deftly and delicately, honing her skills perfectly, but never losing her balance as she had so innocently earlier. Still tilting and tipping and swooning away her soul, she steeped into a deeper trance. Above us the faded moon, etched slightly upon space, smiled. The jangled music ebbed away. We were overjoyed; we nailed it. But, as I had anticipated, the inevitable happened: Spring's father roared up in a pickup.

His voice rattled like the shaking of gravel. "Oh, no you don't! You plotted against me. You know that I had forbidden Spring to dance. She shouldn't be here. And worse, now you made her disobey me, her own father. She sided with you-against me. Now all you've done is to make sure she won't dance again. Never, if I can help it."

Everyone was stunned. As he stormed away with his saddened daughter, I called out in silence, good-bye, Spring! What a dark good-bye.

Quietly the children dispersed.

Andy said, "Lionel, I'm sorry this happened. You tried to make a better film and you did. But maybe you tried too hard. Still, there's no doubt in my mind we have the climax you wanted. I am glad you got it. It's a winner."

"Thanks, especially coming from you. Now all I feel is sick."

"I understand-because of Spring. What happened between the two of them would have happened anyway. You really didn't change anything, so don't take it so hard. And, besides, I believe Spring will continue to dance."

"Yes, I know she'll always be a dancer. But I had no right to take advantage of her. I made my film special, but at what price? One thing consoles me. Spring's great dance really moved me. It has graced my life and I believe it will also grace the lives of others. That's my hope."

THE MASTER

A THOUSAND EYES SCANNED THE countryside and then riveted on one spot. On the hill was the house, a plain house of logs and stones, perched on a clearing devoid of trees and stones. As mirrored in the myriad eyes, smoke and trash and toys and clotheslines and broken wooden steps cluttered around the house. Intruders had chosen to live next to wild neighbors on the grassy slope and within the ring of trees. Sounds rang out often: Sally, Pop, Mamma, come-you-boys, and Lance and Hoadle, and always the sound Hoadle connected with other sounds, as if linking all the odd bits together.

The Hoadles had only Lance and each other. Kirt, the father, was strong and wrestled with trees for the logging company. Sally tended to the house, and eleven-year-old Lance was just getting around to being a schoolboy. School seemed to linger thirty miles away and claimed no jurisdiction on the rough-hewn land. But Lance had been long ago fitted to the idea school, and once the idea had got him, it was a matter of course that he would be ushered along. Sally saw to that.

Before and beyond school lay the land where Lance played. He craved games and worked hard at them, keeping his own private score. Although he was without other children for companions, Lance completely amused himself, never once conscious of his uniqueness. Always serious, the solitary boy sought to prove his importance.

Sally had let him have an old pellet gun of her father's, one made in England that came in a specially fitted box with thousands of pellets. The air rifle was powerful enough to tear a tiny hole through three thick magazines, which was one of the first experiments Lance tried. Sally watched to see that he was careful and he was, even to the point of dedication, and every night he performed the ritual of cleaning the gun. Sally liked his emerging manhood, and his gun took Lance out of the house.

The games he played involved a cosmos of creatures. He hammered at ants with piston rapidity and left in his wake a staggered, wasted army. Then there were crickets which intrigued him because quite often they escaped him, more often than he escaped from his gloomy mother or from his father's dull, tired presence. Playing with toys again, Sally thought, as he performed outside.

Lance could detect a cricket jumping in the brown brush a pace away and sight the velvet flutter of a butterfly as it reeled low over growths and grasses. In his mind he sang a patter, "Come on, come," and once the creature obeyed, then, "No, no, you don't escape," and the gun confirmed that point. Instantly afterwards, "Yes, I have you now," and the thing shot would dangle dead. If he aimed off course he would cry, "A miss! A miss!"

The boy's emotional development made decided strides in the case of birds. Birds plump with hearts beating. Charting a bird trajectory gave Lance bravado. He would shout or scream as he pierced the fleshy chest, turning its feathers into a crimson mat. Nothing could equal harvesting the skies of its riches. Thus the blended orioles, red robins, contrasty magpies, yellow flickers, golden finches, emblazoned pheasants and the iron league of hawks and eagles were eliminated. Lance stomped the fields and meadows. Sally and Kirt saw dead birds occasionally but did not pay much attention to them. Lance neither tried to conceal his hunting nor did he discuss it with them, which meant to them that his interests were transitory, and thankfully school was approaching. As to Lance's view of his parents, they were just stronger, more enduring animals with sentiment, dedicated to restraining him and rendering him dutiful, all the while caging him with loving licks.

Soon he mastered birds and from them he advanced on through mice, rats, squirrels, rabbits and gophers to badgers, skunks and raccoons. Lance was possessed by the little gamesters' combination of fleet strength and cagey endurance. Had they larger dimension, they would compete in stature with the other, more significant species. None of the group begged to live or looked hangdog the way his mother would when she pleaded her commands to him, being so sorry, so wise, so righteous only for his infinite welfare. But the animals never figured that way. They knew what was their due. They realized the inevitable and irreconcilable reality.

Lance believed he understood the nature of each animal; the mouse, furtive and yet pressing; the larger circumspect rat, bumptious and brash when at bay; the badger, tough and mean, controlling upper ground as the gopher does down under. The rabbit, who never followed a path, was avidly appreciated by Lance and didn't let him down. Running on long-femured thumping legs and crashing into the brush willy-nilly, it taught Lance many of his tricks about gun sighting off-angle tuned to the animal's speed.

It hit Lance to feel sorry for the animals, but the blood-brimming beasts never allowed for that. He was learning too much, he was performing perfectly. Besides, his and their blood smoothed on deep, ancient lines that did not involve humility or guilt. The animals were simply living and dying. It was his humanity that he was trying to shed.

Lance understood that school was inevitable and his present days were momentary. In fact, Lance thought that Sally and Kirt understood a great deal more of his killings than they let on and that they believed that school would process him into its regularities and introduce suitable boys and games. At dinner he was fearful of the dangerous words about him which spread from mother to father and father to mother and snapped back to him. In response, he slightly protested and mumbled inaudibly under his breath, merely to placate them, and his parents with resignation would gloss over him, as if he had replied with an expected confession and apology. It was delicately balanced tedium.

So far his game had taken him only around the environs of his house. But there were the big animals in the forest and Lance was ready for them. Kirt and Sally next saw Lance with Kirt's gun. He was remarkably at ease with it, as if it was a part of him. It replaced the pump gun, and he was now a master hunter, ready for higher attainments. The doe, with luminous black orbs for eyes, and the antlered buck, bulging flanks of muscle on brittle, slender legs, seduced Lance through his gun sight and he killed.

So the earth spun out its inner lining for the boy, unraveling its hidden booty as he pierced its living secrets. No spoor went undetected. The one trouble he encountered was in disposing of the carcasses. Lance dug into the hillsides and flatlands and ritualized his kills, for to him the shrines attested to his prowess and mysterious deer-power. Mounds sprang up, marring the countryside. Lance had no need to notch his gun.

He could tell that this was going to be a good day simply because he asked that it be so. He would find the invincible and contest it and in the end conquer it. He never doubted, nor did he lack fear, but rather he tantalized it.

One day he found a dead opossum lying near a trail. The beast lay there in some former agony, with his long pink lip line gashed by harsh and grotesque teeth. Its grizzled death was no accident. A paw of a superior animal had smashed him, leaving his carcass tainted, little meat on small bones with a grisly snout.

Abruptly, a bat-like cry, a sharp nip of high piercing sound pricked the air. It was a sound he had heard before but had never quite connected to its source. His body converted into flawless movement. All the hours of hunting crowded into this moment. Through thickets, leaf by leaf, Lance made his path. He regarded the way twigs and branches moved in the wind and how they hung by their own inanimate weight, as he turned and twitched them back to their place in order to conceal his passage. Soon he saw foxes, a family of reds playing on a dell. Lance frowned because he could not conceive of a tactic which would enable him to kill one big, fine parent without losing the other. The shot ripped and one fox spurted blood and dropped dead, and its mate made off. Disappointed, he fired again. The once jocular yipping and yelping of the cubs changed into wails and whimpers. The cubs had disintegrated into a heap of entrails.

He had realized that the female had seen him before he shot her and uttered a noiseless cry, triggering her mate's singular escape-momentous to Lance. All that he had seen of the male's leap was a bewildering rush of motion, while somehow between his teeth a cub was latched. Lance had checked and counted his kill and he was one cub short.

Still unfulfilled, Lance continued on his quest. He found large tracks leading up an incline strewn with big jumbled rocks and trailing onto a higher slope. The tracks terminated in the hillside. Above him, dark and menacing, was a cave. The tracks had ended when the cave leaned over them. The beast was inside.

The cave tormented him because he could do nothing but wait. Perhaps the brave act would be to storm the cave while firing his gun. But the growing darkness forced his hand. He crawled closer, leveled his body out flat and threw in a few rocks. He was afraid of the black inside, and he wondered if his bluff to frighten the animal would succeed. But the hard, composed, little man tingled with admiration and worship when he heard the body sounds within, the brushing and scraping of a big animal in alarm.

Of being afraid-which both beast and boy were-there was no issue except who would confront whom first. As he approached, he took careful note of all possible protection for himself outside the cave. There was a large boulder behind to which he could retreat. He hesitated to make sure his feet were going forward; he seemed defied by the cave. He crossed the nether boundary between worlds. As he entered the cave he heard the launching and a miniature cascade of dirt and pebbles. With animal instinct he slammed himself to earth.

A rippled surge exploded and the monster leaped to break out and soared over the boy's sprawling form. Lance sprang up. He saw nothing, feeling only his own failure. He was perilously wedged in the cave's opening.

He emerged to hear a rustle, a meaningful one, and adroitly he went for the rock-defense he had already scouted out. Looking for cover, he found the panther already there, waiting for him. The tawny god spat at him, his star-splayed eyes shone, and he sprang. Lance fired without aiming and the whole hulk of muscle spasms crashed behind him. The gun was torn away by a stroke of its paw and banged down on the rock. Lance was toppled over as the lion powered on, churned the ground and died.

He gazed at the wake of commotion and havoc and at the ageless, sleeping, great spread of beast, the paws drooping and pads turned outward towards the head, now a poised lantern with the light extinguished. The boy glowed with passion and peace and welcomed the darkness entering the dusk. But a sadness overtook him. He could see a marred form, a friend's tragedy. He let out a splintery cry before he suppressed it. He reached down, weighty and solemn, as he gathered up the broken gun. His fortune had run its course.

To his parents his battered gun and late arrival spoke for themselves. School would begin the day after tomorrow, and he was trapped. One day of his free self remained and with his gun injured. At dinner Sally suggested that for his last day, a Sunday, he should remain at home with them and stay out of trouble. This spurred Kirt on to make plans to be with the boy. His parents continually reiterated that the gun was no more. They were no longer anxious or grave or overwhelmingly paternal, and they made no attempt to conceal their welcome for their child's coming civilized transfiguration. Their haphazard concern for him was not enough to affect him. Throughout all their messing with his affairs he realized that they had no conception of how he felt about his past paradise.

Alone in his room Lance enjoyed the balmy night and kept the windows open. Preoccupied with the day's events, he thought about his gun and decided to restore it. Resuscitating the rifle was easier than he had imagined. He had an assortment of screws and bolts with which he easily repaired it. Except for some dents and a chip off the gunstock, the duo of boy and gun was restored.

During the repair, the wind abruptly soughed, sounding like a wild snort, and the atmosphere sharply activated. A summer storm, he thought, until the swishing and swooping outdoors made this assessment untenable. Carrying his gun to the window, he saw a procession of flitting and floating eyes slip by, and black forms, suddenly made light and black again, careened and wove around the house. Flashes of illumination revealed a searing battlement of animals he had known, fixing their honest bestiality on him. They were a dare, an effrontery. He considered dashing among them and working his gun and retaliating with brazen bullets, but he knew Sally and Kirt would stop him, so he went to bed.

Before the rooster awoke, Lance dressed and with his gun strode outside and away. If Sally and Kirt had expected him to parcel himself off to them on his only day left, they were mistaken. Any one day of the countless that would ebb by later would do for them. And for the animals? He reserved respect for his inferiors within a walled-up hatred. They did not acknowledge his dominance.

Soon Lance was far from the house. No chirping soared because there were no birds to sing. The anthills were not trembling with ants. No bees or crickets or flies provided a veil of sound. He thought he saw a butterfly, but an elusive shadow flicked for what it was. When the field mice didn't perk up and oscillate and the cottontails didn't startle and bolt, then the boy lit up. He began searching the wavy undergrowth for a snake, which oddly was the least likely creature to be found. He stopped and peered down a gopher hole but realized he was being ridiculous. The wind was stirring warm and alive, but no eagle meshed with it. With relief he noticed a pack rat nest with its jumble of odds and ends of the wide world, including one of his empty rifle shells. Signs existed of obscure tracks, crusts of excrement and residue of loose hair and fallen feathers, but nowhere could he find any living things.

Lance trod on his shadow. In a pond he saw himself.

His gun, like a magnetic pole, began to tremble. He followed its directions and an animal took shape where the gun had nodded. A bobcat loomed in his gaze and he greeted it reverently. The animals had not forsaken him; they were his to master.

Lance took slow aim at the sleek bobcat and shot, but there was no sign of a kill. Then he caught a beaver in his vision, sighted and fired, but examining the stream there was no beaver. He was more baffled than before. He could explain a drought of animals but not a mirage.

When he saw an elk standing among a drove of deer, he swore love on its huge body. A giant cravat of yellow mushrooming hair hung from its throat and a headdress of bone latticework waved from its head. Unquestionably the leader, the elk rotated its massive quarters. It had strayed north, to be dominated by Lance. He coolly dispatched his shot. He then numbly watched the elk start and lope away, while the deer followed, bobbing their rumps.

The tramp home was the most sickening. He had to inhale silence and humiliation and each was insufferable. Sally and Kirt would be generous with welcomes, even though he had hurt them, and he would detest their kindness. Would they ever be honest with themselves about him? But whatever. It was this, his last day out, that haunted him. When he got home, he could not tell his parents there was no game and he could not say he didn't hunt, because he couldn't form the necessary words and because no one would believe him.

A quilt of strangeness settled over him. The air thickly condensed in the spaces around his legs and arms and slowed his steps into hard going. As he walked, he sensed a carpet of movements and sounds darkly flowing, sliding along as he dragged his feet. He would abruptly stop and the subdued, slow shuffle and slithering would cease. He would step out and the insistent darting noises would sound again. He began to make time. He was not far from his house, Sally's house, Kirt's house, and not the enemy's house. He gauged that once he reached the grassy slope before his home the phantoms would dissipate. But they remained. The seething movements and sounds grew wilder and more fierce. As he ran, Lance found himself lunging across some magic barrier. While he increased his speed, blasting figures dove and swarmed past him and over him and through his running. Yet he made the grassy slope—which he had calculated he would—and several yards further.

It was then that he was ringed by his fellow players in the fields. He could see the familiar roster. Even a bear awaited him. With disdain distilled with rage, Lance stared fiercely back. Staring at them without blinking, a technique which had never failed him, did not melt their steady gaze or provide him any extra strength. Rather their eyes battered him and changed from puzzlement to no fear to blatant aggression. Lance's gaze broke futilely from their eyes and he decided to stand on his patience, patience that was unique to man. But so did the fox and the badger and the mountain lion, for they were not pressed or destined to be at any place and never had been.

Soon the boy realized that he must turn to his ultimate resort: to speak and be man. He explained to the throng of jackrabbits and the coyote and the deer that they were relegated to their place by precisely such a phenomenon as himself. They had felt fear of him before but were now exceeding the natural boundaries that distinguished men from brutes. They should desist, but the animals only shifted their eyes. He was now the one hunted. Sensing a knot of despair that had begun to hobble him, Lance asked for grace and forgiveness with a dash of pity, and love found his lips. With that he quickly moved and tried to push his way out. But the animals did not heed. They defied him and closed their ranks. Lance stepped back and took measure of them. He eyed his empty gun, grabbed it by the barrel and, swinging it, wielded it up high to strike.

Moaning and wailing gushed out. The badger positioned his scythe-like claws and struck, the deer's hooves descended like crushing rocks, the fox snipped at the arteries where the blood coursed and the rear claws of the mountain lion raked deep with the force of coiled and hidden springs. Still the boy deployed his gun stock with happy savagery. Lance was in true fettle now, smashing the butt so hard that it fused with the animals. He was joyous among the throng, at last cognizant that he and they were equal, exchanging brave strokes of fulfillment. But Lance could not account for their survival; he could not find an injured beast.

Surprised, he was downed and muffled under the weight of writhing bodies. He hurt. He was entwined in a cocoon of pounding blows, and for the first time he experienced the long pain that comes as the prelude to one's doom.

Then it changed. The fighting thudded over him and away. At the end, when instinct and reflex could hardly respond and at last flickered out, then his scorching disgust of fear branded itself over his wounds and bruises which led to a dying, the death, his death. He held, until the eagle dropped down from the sky and its talons calipered on his face and cranked it backwards, until the snowy ermine slashed his tendons and the mole nibbled on his toes, and then the whole wave of pulsating flesh collapsed on the boy.

The boy was never found. The jumbled events remained unexplained. And the thousand eyes that had watched the countryside now drummed over it, content and satisfied.

FINAL DECLENSION

ON FEBRUARY 8TH, 1994, AT 8:00 A.M., Dora Templeton was preparing to greet her friend, Evette Pardo. Two daughters and a husband had taken a toll on her once fine, clean-featured face. At this moment she had barely enough time to contemplate the pleasure she would have in receiving Evette as a loyal guest and, beyond that, a dear soul. Dora's husband had just left their home, a two-story, 1910 Edwardian brick house she thought much too large for them since their two daughters had married. If Evette was a friend (and she definitely was), she was a friend to Dora alone and not a social companion shared with Dora's husband. She was in fact her favorite friend and finally her only pupil, who for twenty-five years had been visiting her regularly for instruction in ancient Greek studies. Twenty-five years of Evette driving every Monday from her South Denver residence. Now at seventy-eight, she was still braving the crowded highways in order to nestle into the rich, book-lined study of her mentor and teacher. Dora had asked Evette if the drive was too strenuous and she answered, "What else would I do if I didn't come to your class? There is no point in doing anything if I don't get my lesson from you. No point at all." Because to

Evette, a high school Latin teacher back east before she arrived in Denver and later retired, the whole point of her past life was to decline nouns, pronouns and adjectives. She arrived as a capable, dedicated teacher who cared for students, and in her absorption with them, she never managed to marry. Instead, she eloped with her special classical Latin poets. Evette was one of a group of sixteen teachers who had decided years ago to study Greek. Throughout her teaching career, she had immersed herself in Latin and now in retirement, she firmly declared that she wished to concentrate on learning the Greek language. Dora, forty-five at the time, was teaching Greek at Denver University when she was chosen by the group as its instructor. And so began the odyssey of adventure and learning where she encountered a varied list of characters: a doctor of philosophy who started an institution to revere Ayn Rand, a real doctor, the ubiquitous lawyer, the merchant and among the assemblage a lost neo-fascist whom she disliked but whose wretched qualities she also pitied (plus, he, too, was loyal). Yet when he faded away, as the others had before him, out emerged Evette, the star in the pursuit of knowledge, the remaining student to keep the Greek torch alive. In order to teach, Dora basically needed only one student and fortunately she ended up with Evette. She sighed at the crowded, exhausting scene of rich segments of her life that she had just visualized and proceeded to brew the herbal tea Evette literally craved. Her hair, she realized, almost matched Evette's in its grayness. They were both small, active individuals but were slowing down, especially Evette. Now it was simply she and Evette who engaged, who crossed, rendezvoused, calculated, and who stimulated each other in a fusion of intellectual bonding. She likened herself to a master scribe in harmony with her apprentice. Even so, it was a long, hard process, Dora conceded, to transform her partner's scan of perfunctory thinking into connected thoughts wired with vision, to probe far and beyond the ordinary, cursory cant. In her patient, undulating voice she asked Evette early on who was the hero of the *Iliad*, and she responded that Hector took the honor, since he was a family man with family values. Exasperated, she questioned whether Evette could penetrate to the deeper meanings. In this case, Achilles was the obvious hero. Evette's aged body stiffened and her mouth became hard and tight as she struggled to understand these core issues of Homer and the Greek tragedies that she had never before fathomed. To admit that Evette perhaps could not glean the verities of history, race and myth but could just translate word by word the literary works into Greek was not to Dora an admission of failure. Rather, it attested to the woman's arduous perseverance, stemming from her conservative, orthodox upbringing. The Greek classics were hot, contentious stuff, Dora chuckled, a gauntlet of thieves, liars, womanizers, perpetrators of infanticide, patricide and matricide, avengers, woman-batterers and maybe panders; hot coals too brilliant for Evette to easily handle. A refined yet primitive horde to Evette, the Greeks were almost unmanageable. Once, when Dora spoke of the sexual innuendoes in the Greek plays, Evette painfully jumped up and replied with prissy heat, "Dora Templeton, you're like everyone else–all you think about is sex." Dora smiled. Certainly their relationship, or even that of her and her husband, dealt little with sex. At that moment the kettle whistled, signaling the boiling tea was ready, and the red flower-decorated porcelain cups stood by to be scalded. Dominating over her kitchen, Dora recalled that Evette often enjoyed sipping her tea and eating scones, which she had forgotten to buy. Today they would work on Virgil. She knew Evette was anxious to continue with the last book of Virgil's *Aeneid*, the Roman classic Evette preferred when she taught high school, even though Dora tried to tell her that, compared to the first book, it was second-rate Virgil and thus considerably inferior to the great Greeks. The tea was cooling when she noticed that it was past lesson time. Evette was never one to be late; in fact, she was usually slightly early, eager to begin. Dora sat down to think, placing the hot cup to her lips and down again. Evette hadn't called, but she wouldn't; she never had. Possibly the traffic or her medication intervened. Dora put a tea cozy over the pot to keep it hot and got up to look out the window. Nothing. Surely it would be appropriate, she considered, if she telephoned Evette in a few minutes to inquire if she had left, to clear all concerns. Dora found it difficult to wait. She fingered the telephone, started to dial it, hesitated and then decided to continue. The telephone rang, linking her to Evette. At the fifth ring she was about to give up, figuring that Evette was on her way, when a male voice came on the line. She believed she had the wrong number and almost hung up but blurted out that she was attempting to reach a Miss Pardo and was sorry to bother the man. "Not at all," he told her. "You have the right number, although I am afraid to inform you that my sister, Evette, died two days ago from a stroke, and I am here to make the proper arrangements. Are you a friend?" Dora jerked the receiver away while the voice droned. Then she brought it back to her mouth. "I am sorry to hear that. Thank you." And in confusion she hung up. She gazed at the tea pot and the saucers and the absence of scones, and she took up her volume of Virgil and turned to where she and Evette were to read. She moaned quietly, "She would never understand how poorly Virgil, even at his best, ranks with Homer. Never." She closed the book, laid it gently on a table and went to the kitchen and slowly poured the tea into the sink.

COWS

HE ALWAYS MADE ONE MISTAKE.

He didn't err with his wife Macedonia, whom he married after the Hitler war, when he settled next to his tough old mother on deeded land, or when he produced two sons and two daughters. But he always screwed up when he messed with cows. Why couldn't he understand that a cow is a cow and not more than a cow? The bad pun that he had been udderly foolish with bovines since he had brought four females to his ranch in Costillo, New Mexico, was painfully true. To Narciso, four animals qualified as a herd. He likened raising cows to modern day business. First, an investor creates operating stock in an enterprise, which in his case consisted of four cows. As further capitalization is added, meaning the reproduction of new cows, the business would increase its future shares of stock and their respective value, while earning the shareholder greater dividends. Although Narciso hazily believed in the theory of financial success, he was not so sure his barnyard commodities would cooperate.

His cow-splurge began some time ago, when his black hair had no gray streaks, his mustache didn't droop along with his six-foot frame and his gut didn't bulge beyond his belt. Regardless, as a heavy equipment operator, he, Narciso Taverez, was one of the few respected elders in Costillo, and he still maintained ownership of four cows, one-two-three-four vacas.

He treated them like pets. They were his darlings and they required care. He pastured them on land he leased on the mountain and they grew silky and fat, which pleased him. After providing them with a quiet adolescence, he arranged with a neighbor who owned a bull to let his cows pasture in the man's field. Narciso anticipated calf dividends.

The summer was arid with brittle grass and a howling, oppressive winter struck early. The cows withered. One had a false pregnancy and the others ran around ragged and looked like sorry cases for an animal shelter. Narciso tried to nurse them back to their former state but they never recovered. In a foul mood he sold them for a pittance and purchased another four. They were the same White Face breed. Nothing right happened: they became sick with brackish water, broke the fence, ran away and were secretly sequestered by a devious neighbor, and they got skinned up on the barbwire fence. They courted a bad fate.

At long last Narciso felt like divesting himself of cows.

The mare he then acquired was truly wondrous, a fast, smooth runner, quick to respond, and when ridden on long stretches didn't breathe heavily. Narciso was a winner. The mare made him smile when he rode her and allowed him to overcome the layer of seriousness which often smothered his face. He relaxed. But his grandchildren could not learn to ride such an active horse. They must be considered. So he fretted.

His new urge was to exchange the mare for a gentler mount. Inexplicably, he failed to carry out this purpose and somehow managed to trade the mare for four small cows, as he understood the deal, four young animals. Adding to the complete bewilderment of his family and neighbors, he spotted a young, springy bull, also owned by the man with the cows, and proceeded to buy it for five hundred dollars. As amazed as they were, the villagers admitted that, given the weight of the evidence, Narciso had concocted an excellent trade—one horse got him four cows and five hundred dollars snagged him a young bull. Obviously the beast sold cheap because it must have defects. It was eight months old, born and raised in the seller's mountain pasture, and only during the last two days, when it had been brought down by truck and trailer and traded, had it been exposed to the slightest veneer of the ranching world. In short, the bull was too young to release and too old to change. It was wild. A wild bull. Clearly, that was the reason he was disposed of at an advantageous price.

But why, the town inhabitants pondered, why would Narciso wish to raise cows again after he had dispensed with them for a fine mare, and how he could forget his past failures? What could he gain? Although Narciso wondered, too, he prided himself that he was a good trader, and moreover, he had fallen back to cows because he liked them; they were his first love. Later he discovered that what he thought had been sold to him as young cows were actually midgets, veritable dwarfs.

To haul the animals to his rented mountain pasture involved a sturdy truck and a good-sized trailer. That morning, with his cowboy dude son, Atencio, and his young son-in-law, Candido, helping him steer the herd into the corral and then through the chute and into the trailer, Narciso felt the sun had risen for him. Not the least of the reasons for his raised spirits was the arrival of the bull, his bull, which he must admit did not disappoint him. His livestock fortunes, he predicted, could only improve.

The lead cow started toward the corral, trailed by the herd. Narciso chuckled as he remembered the nursery rhyme about Mary's lamb, the lamb was sure to go, only it was a bull. But the bull did not follow. In fact, it balked, became jumpy, jittery, and backed away. When the men attempted to hem it in by crowding it toward the net of corral fences, it darted away, nimbly avoiding their efforts, and broke free to the outside field. The men swiftly pursued and the bull, like a magnet, pulled them up the mesa and down, down and up. It was as if they were playing an endless game of insane tag. Winded, the men threatened obscene consequences, hurled screaming oaths and swore and swore unkind thoughts as they streamed by up and down in disarray. Then they stopped, their chests heaving in agony, their bodies smeared with sweat. Their quarry likewise stopped.

Narciso now realized that the bull could only be regarded as quarry and no longer as reliable livestock. Disgusted and shamed by the mistake he had made, he yelled out that he was at fault and should have known that a bull of eight months, bred in the mountains, would only turn out wild. How could he be other than an "hombre estupido?" A stupid man. "Loco!" he bellowed, "El toro es loco!"

Forming a human dragnet, the men reorganized and carefully advanced. At the same time they waved their hands in the air, hooted, whistled, shrieked and jumped up and down, effectively forcing the bull to drop down the mesa toward the corral. It stepped forward gingerly, tentatively. Narciso quickly moved in back of it, while his helpers went to each side of the gate. The bull paused, mired in distrust and doubt, and abruptly charged into the enclosure where the lead cow and brethren were patiently waiting.

The men immediately closed the gate. Round and round coursed the bull until finally it stopped, stood still and eyed the cows as they passed through the chute. To Narciso, its eyes crackled with wily calculation as it sized up the situation. The open chute seemed to offer the only passageway to freedom. The bull plunged through the chute and into the trailer that was hitched to the truck. Instantly it realized its error and tried to jump over the trailer railing. With equal agility Narciso lassoed it and tied its head to the lower trailer rails. The bull struggled and attempted to rear up its head. Two oversize hand-forged iron weights, a pound each, were attached to the sharp tips of its perfectly straight and especially dangerous horns in order to bend and shape them into rounded curves.

During this operation, Atencio held back and watched. Because he wore fancy clothes, many thought he was above the rough and messy job involved in raising cattle. But, in reality, he didn't wish to see the animals suffer and he particularly disliked watching the bull tied down, its eyes rolling in terror.

Narciso drove the truck across sheltered fields interspersed with adobe dwellings and arrived at the canyon's mouth, which led up to the summer mountain pasture. Upon release the lead cow first climbed the steep trail, when the bull in a burst streaked past her and assumed command of the herd. Relieved, the men grinned and kicked up their heels.

Winter came and talk about the bull reigned supreme in the bar, cafe, firehouse, poker parlor and most of the private homes in Costillo. Narciso and his pet bull. The joke's on-who has the bull by the horns, the bull or Narciso? The ranchers contended the ranch hands were lucky to stop the animal before it reached the open pasture above the corral, where they would still be chasing it. Dubbing it Loco, Narciso must have been plenty angry to give it that name. For a young steer maybe the name Poco Loco would be better-just a little crazy. But could the vacqueros get it down, and if they could, could it be trained? Some wild mustangs have been ridden like ordinary horses. But was Loco actually too loco?

Narciso hiked up the mountain a few times to check on the cows and to take them a block of salt. He had a good lead cow that he could trust to guard the calves and guide the others to the best grasses, streams and salt licks, and in September or just before winter she would show the group the right way home. When the middle of September arrived, Narciso decided not to wait for the herd to materialize but to go into the mountains and bring them back himself. He met them halfway and then understood why they were late. The lead cow had twisted her foot and was limping. Narciso spied the rest of the group but not the bull. He climbed higher and found it, holding back and nervously distancing itself from the cows. But a transformation had taken place.

The young bull loomed big, enormous to be sure, spreading out in all directions, filled solid with coiled bunches of tight knots and yet surprisingly lithe for an animal its size. It had flawless control over every quick step it took-an amazing talent for a beast so large. He faced a twelve-hundred pound masterpiece of its kind. And certainly testy. Almost before Narciso moved, the bull seemed to be everywhere at once, hooking back to the mountains, then thunderously rushing down and circling the cows, causing them to panic. Narciso thought that this was the creature so well qualified it could define the word rapido, it was that fast; the bull moved like the long-legged wolf.

But the bull looked odd: one of the weights on its horns was sheared off, giving it the bizarre, surreal look of a satyr. Continually maneuvering the beast, Narciso prodded and pressed it downward, while he stumbled on the harsh path. He was grateful for the stream frothing next to the trail because being near it made him feel better about his work and himself. The bull ripped ahead in jerks, even bounces, and Narciso noticed its muscles moved like inner gears. The bull was heading for the lower reaches, where on the left appeared a tangled brace of stout trees and on the right a cliff which ran straight down and out of the canyon; in order to avoid capture in the open fields it had to circumvent both. Narciso hoped to contain it to a leisurely pace along the side of the cliff wall.

However, the bull devised its own scheme, and exploding past the excited cows, it accelerated and crashed into the lead cow down the trail, knocking her over into a crevice below. The cow landed between two large boulders, and the more she struggled the further in she became wedged. Worse, Narciso saw that she had either broken some ribs or perhaps her back. Alone, and with the remainder of his stock at stake, he had to continue. Anyway, she would soon die from shock.

A more costly blow could not have befallen Narciso. Enraged, he clenched his right fist and shoved it into heaven's face and he vehemently shrieked, "No es loco, es diablo! Diablo malo!" A bad devil. Not letting up for a second, Narciso kept behind the bull when they came in sight of the canyon's entrance. The bull hesitated a moment, vainly searching for an escape route, groping, when with a spurt it instinctively veered to the right and into a ragged ravine that rose up towards the cliff and continued some distance above the trail. The last exit.

Was it possible the bull had the power to will whatever it wanted to take place, Narciso wondered? Was Dios on its side or his? A God for a bull? Whatever. This could only be a strange God, indeed. This miracle ravine, more like a wash, had hardly existed to him. Although the bull had won a delay by losing itself in the ravine, Narciso had the mental comfort of knowing that the arroyo would end at a wall and the bull must soon return. By keeping himself uphill from the bull, he could force it down the ravine and as it crossed back on to the trail, he could coerce it to leave the canyon. The beast, thwarted by finding its route blocked, came cascading back down the wash, with Narciso bravely positioning himself above it and to its right. When it reached the trail, Narciso began throwing rocks at the toro in frustration. He pelted it so hard that he clumsily fell forward, and completely off balance, he awkwardly threw a stone down on his foot. The bull brushed off the bombardment, and probing to discover a way out of its confinement, it paused again. Ignoring the canyon exit, it launched off, prancing like a deer across the trail and stream, and undaunted, violently hurled itself into the thick density of ponderosa and Douglas pine, which was reinforced with a mesh of scrub oaks and willows.

Lunging, ramming, churning, battering, ripping, uprooting and to Narciso's mind probably cursing, the bull plowed into all resistance and powered through to the other side. It vanished into the mountains. Narciso stood there hopeless and helpless. He supposed the brute was laughing. Tired and anticipating darkness, he decided to call it quits. He had already lost his most valuable cow-an expensive venture. With the remainder of the herd traumatized by the turmoil of events, he dejectedly headed home.

A cow had gone down and a bull had gone up; this was the conclusion the town folk drew from the stories brought down from the mountain. A bull leaping like a deer. Magical. Magical and evil at the same leap. Pity the lead cow. Up there where the snows swirl on the peaks, emotions get mixed up in the high thin air. Funny things happen. Spirits can take other forms. Deer mate with wolves. A young bull raised in the mountains may crave blood and howl at the moon. Fellow spirits, gone mad, run together.

It nagged Narciso that the bull thrived on the mountain, totally free and out of place, challenging the natural working order. He knew it shouldn't be there, shouldn't mingle with the wild creatures. It was just becoming wilder and wilder and day by day harder to bring in. Narciso could feel its stubborn willfulness spreading in its brain, enveloping its heart. It was time to grab the demon.

With his son-in-law, Candido, Narciso attacked the mountain. He didn't take Atencio because he couldn't square his cowboy dude clothes with the rigors of winter and Candido worked best as an all-purpose hand.

The bull could be anywhere. Since it was a mild winter, it did not need to graze at a lower range but could stay up higher and survive. At first Candido asked to try his luck alone, but after confronting a cutting, chilling wind he came back exhausted. His lungs hurt from taking in the cold air. Still, he discovered signs of bighorn mountain sheep or maybe something else unusual. A bit further on they found large, wide tracks in the snow, positioned at fifteen-foot intervals, one after another inclining steeply downward. It was as if some strange, hopping monster made tracks disfiguring the slope. Suddenly they looked up. Fleeing before them, the bull jumped, sprang and bounded, soaring high and clear from rock to crag to pinnacle, thrusting and jamming its front legs straight down before it, hard and stiff, sufficiently bracing itself to absorb the shock of its airy landings. Almost three quarters of a ton of whirling acrobatics speeding from jump to jump. The men followed, grappling with the timberline and its mass of huge evergreen trees. But the bull couldn't be found. It had disappeared into thin air.

Candido had to relieve himself and squatted low in a crevice. Glancing over the terrain from his ground level, he unexpectedly caught a glimpse of the bull hiding just beneath the line of trees. Barely buckling his belt, he ran out and with Narciso chased the lunatic. Down, careening, catapulting, surging, nimbly hurdling over the rock-route, the bull flung itself away in a skyward dance, away, far from its pursuers. The game, Narciso complained, playing its piss-poor game of racing up and down, down and up with cunning, he couldn't half match. He could hardly keep the enemy in sight; shit! The haggard men passively watched the phantom effortlessly dash toward the summit. The bull was always out of their reach. Both of them burned, tightened up inside, scowled, dropped their heads, shrugged and squeezed out an abortive laugh. They felt silly.

Narciso came down without the bull. The village teased him. No bull; poor Narciso. He couldn't cope. The bull ruled. The joke circulating around was, if you need good cows, especially a bull, avoid Narciso.

Finally, Macedonia intervened. She told her husband that he saw the bull wrong. It is not a bull anymore but some piece of the mountain with deep roots there. Can you tame or capture a mountain? There are things no one can do. No more should Narciso go after the bull or he'd find trouble.

He should listen. Narciso shook his head and countered. It made no difference what she said. The bull was still a bull, for which he had paid good money, and he, the owner, planned to get it back. Now the bull is big with folds of meat and is worth more. And the cows, they can't have calves without his bull. Besides, it's a man's life.

Macedonia agreed with him-she always agreed when he put down his reasons carefully-but she protested: his arguments didn't work this time. It's not about arguments, she said; you can't reason with a bull. This wild bull kicks down all his arguments.

It snowed. Each night Narciso clumped in his special chair facing the immutable fire, while the bull continually remained with him, prancing in the edges of his mind. Loco, he pondered, who's more loco, he or the bull? Yes, it might not be right for a bull to run on the mountain with deer and elk, mountain sheep and, he conjectured, a few wolves or at least wild dogs. He didn't think so. But why did he mind? Because the bull outsmarted him? Or rather fooled him? No, outsmarted him. Did he view the bull as a rival? To a degree, but not all the time. What bothered him most was that the bull up there pawing the mountain didn't fit. It was not in its correct place-with him and the cows on the ranch, where it belonged. Instead it lingered in the dark and wild. He, Narciso, must remedy that.

The next day, quite early, Narciso left. He admitted Macedonia had good instincts. He was dumb to go. The snow banked three feet high and his horse painfully worked through the white stretch of opposition. It came to Narciso that the animal must be wondering why he chose today of all days to ride. Narciso brought his gun with him, and this little bit of stealth he had not told his wife. He took it because if he could just manage to locate the bull, since he couldn't catch it, he would shoot it. At least that way he would have the meat. He would mark where it was and leave it there until the next day, when he would return with two sturdy horses to pack it out. He considered his decision a poor solution at best but he didn't feel bad about it. There was nothing illegal about shooting your own bull.

With no bull in sight, his hopes wilted, and as he hunched along he thought of himself as a splotch of soggy, crusty frijoles, beans half dead, beyond hope. No bull could be seen, only sullen, endless snow. At the mouth of the creek he sensed that he had failed. He was out of control, acting out of desperation. Stepping carefully around a protruding rock, his horse got tangled in a stray willow, lost its footing and tumbled down into the creek, throwing Narciso free. As he landed on his back in the snow, it struck him that this disaster was the proper conclusion to his madness. At the same time, as if in a ballet in slow motion, he watched his horse roll over on its back, fold its legs underneath, and catching itself, push its body up and onto its feet in one miraculous swoop. Narciso lay there happy. His horse had not broken a leg and he wasn't hurt. All the pieces could be put back together again.

Except for one. His best gun lay smashed on a rock, and without inspecting it, he could tell it was hurt, its action bent, shattered, a twenty-two he had hoarded from his World War II days. This underlined a lesson to be learned or a precept he should have absorbed-he shouldn't have taken his gun. He was almost glad that the gun was dead and the bull alive.

Back home, Narciso studied his remaining stunted cows. He now had no stomach for them. He was discouraged. When the news that Narciso contemplated disposing of his herd reached the community, it was received with good humor. He was deemed fickle. One year Narciso loves cows and buys his usual quota of quatro-always four of them. The next he tires of them and wishes them gone. Today is gone time. Tomorrow he might turn to those fancy, hairy animals-llamas-that the new gringos like. Imagine! A whole field of llamas like daisies. Might as well be looking at giraffes.

The day the rumor set in that the missing bull had journeyed down and crossed over onto the Indian Pueblo, land forbidden to trespassers but for the bull a haven, Narciso decided to visit the vet. The vet told him the bull had done its job: two cows would calve in the early spring. Narciso listened without a word, went home and waited. He took the coming births seriously. He carried out his business, reinforced the pig pen, continually tinkered with the fences and sold his bulldozer, but essentially he waited.

But what he wanted to do was seriously worry. A bull, now sixteen hundred pounds, could weigh heavy on anyone's mind. But soon the worrying ended. The smallest cow gave birth to a dead calf, a bull. The vet explained that the calf had a breach. It couldn't be discharged from the mother because one of its legs folded underneath it and the calf got stuck. An accident. The calf had smothered, and afterwards was removed from the cow, which pulled through.

Narciso exploded. To everyone's surprise he turned violent. He cursed, many times stronger than he did at the bull, and raged and stormed, but his friends figured his behavior was a torrent of emotion directed at the bull. Narciso blamed it for killing its calf, his calf. By the bull nagging and scaring the herd and continually disturbing and badgering it, the cows became upset and the babies inside the mothers got mixed up and turned around upside down. The bull had done it. Narciso fumed. Should he get the cow an orphan calf to mother? This had been known to work. Would this help the mother and ease his own anguish? That's all he could do. But six hours later Narciso had changed his mind.

His other cow delivered a healthy bull. The herd at last had a bull to protect it. That's what he cared about. He was content; he had been rewarded. The bull paid him back and he didn't lose any money. Now at peace, he could forget the bull he lost and from this day on concentrate on the bull just born that he could call his own, an idea that comforted him for a long time.

The town took Narciso for granted. After all, it acknowledged, what else could Narciso be but Narciso? Besides being just like a bull-crazy.

CAUGHT

THE HIPPIES ELUDED THEIR TRACKERS for eight days before they were cornered and caught. Now, as prisoners hunched together under the brow of the mountain, they contemplated their eight days of running, dodging, scrambling, ducking, having a ball. Glorious! Raspberries on the bush for picking, staining the teeth of the men crimson, the dark juices splattering their chins and chests as they gobbled down the forbidden fruit. Fat blissful fish sojourning in a full river that looked like a moveable prism. Great groups of trees growling in the wind, rearing their bushiness tall and angry.

Several times they had spotted the Indians at a distance, incessantly pursuing, but they'd managed to escape, using some Indian tricks of their own that these real Indians didn't know. They'd concocted a device employing a fallen tree trunk to catapult themselves onto a high rock so their tracks couldn't be discovered. From there they had peered down, laughing at the hot and frustrated Indians searching for them underneath in a habitat the hippies had screwed up with traps and snares for their own purposes. But finally the state of grace ended. Even in 60,000 acres of wilderness they couldn't ultimately lose their trackers. Maybe they hadn't properly concealed their tracks or completely obliterated their campfires. Who knows? But they had been waylaid and caught.

During this frantic splurge, one of the hippies who had been to college thought about the anthropologists and environmentalists who had taught him about the wilderness and the land. With all their clinical and reverent words they could not half describe what it was like to be hunkered under the jagged promontory of a vibrant mountain, rooted, where parties of deer assembled and where it seemed that the entire animal kingdom appeared-flying, flitting and scurrying in every direction. It was a time of no time, the beginning and end melded feverishly together. Now looking down at the mud slabs of dwellings that comprised the town, his thoughts slithered back through layers of the past where there might have been a beginning.

The hippies had arrived in northern New Mexico, to them a sliver of paradise, in the late sixties on a cultural upswing. Perhaps it would turn out to be a downswing. Anyway, they were there and it didn't matter. However, one hippie thought that something mattered. According to a science book he had read in high school, matter never dissolves completely but changes into something else. So he mattered, he and his band of hippies living in clusters on the open land. They were very hip when they chose to settle away from town and live in the countryside. They camped in a spot above the remote village of Dolores, next to a river so small that, if it were located anywhere else, it would be called a stream. They used the store and trekked along the town's only road to reach neighboring areas, but they didn't participate in the affairs of the village.

The Spanish population was living as if in the 1940s and 1950s, aspiring to the middle class life the hippies were rejecting. The locals professed to worship the divine Kingdom of God, which was bad enough to the newcomers, but worse was the infestation of wall-to-wall carpets, refrigerators, dishwashers and electric ovens. What kind of God had led them to Sears and Roebuck? The hippies laughed at the simple folks who, in their innocence, did not realize they were being duped by the perpetrators of the hated status quo. Their lifestyles were too different to reconcile.

Already insulted by the hippies, the villagers were shocked by the flagrant immorality of the hippies running unclothed in the pastures of the Lord. Enraged, the young men of the neighborhood beat them up and tried to drive them out. Although head-bashing was a crime, the Hispanic police did not intervene. Over time hot tempers managed to cool and the hippies survived.

During that period the hippies were drawn to the Indian Pueblo. A magnetic mountain presided over its two adobe settlements and guarded those below who lived in them. Snuggled beneath the mountain, their cultural identity was unshakable. The hippies respected the Indians who had preserved their realm just for themselves, remote and inviolate, run by mystical rites only the Indians understood. They were drawn by the Pueblo's intangible ties. Sears and Roebuck was not an icon in the Indians' consciousness. The hippies wanted most to live on the Indians' mountain and lose themselves in its secrets. They asked a head honcho of the Pueblo for permission to camp there for a few weeks. He emphatically said no. He refused to give a reason, but turned his back and walked away. Undeterred and determined to do what they wanted, the hippies sneaked past the Pueblo in the dark, heading unseen for the mountain.

But now the present was urgently intruding upon the hippies. They had only believed in the present moment; in this case they were being consumed by it. They were now buried with problems. The Indians who captured them were enraged. Mute, solemn and inwardly focused, they forcibly marched the hippies down the mountain. What few words were spoken were directions and commands such as "stay here" and "don't pee in the stream." Never did the guardians let their captives out of sight. It was easy for the hippies to resist any urge to escape. They knew better. If they should try, the Indians would come crashing down on them like a runaway boulder finding its way down a hillside. Keeping their eyes to the front, they did what they were told. After three days of tension, the Indians sent runners to the Pueblo to inform the tribe of their coming.

The group arrived in the late afternoon in the middle of the Pueblo plaza. Two Indian elders, distinguished by woolen Pendelton blankets wrapped around their waists and flipped over their heads, came over and joined them. The hippies were led through the plaza which was skirted by a series of adobe apartments, some three stories high. They were taken into a room on the ground floor. The roof was supported by darkened logs, and a large hand-adzed wooden table, rimmed by an assortment of chairs, enhanced the graceful emptiness. The hippies were told to sit down.

No one spoke. Time dissolved, seeped out the door. The Indians sat stoically. The hippies feared their growing anger. Finally, one of the elders, rising from his chair, came around to face them.

"You, you, and you," he pointed, his hand trembling, "you should not be here; you don't belong here. We should not have to see you or hear you or smell you. You are not here to us."

Shocked and listening intently, they found it amazing that such a seemingly gentle old man, perhaps partly blind, could be so forbidding and fierce. Each of his words stamped a hot brand of contempt.

An educated man about forty, adjusting his glasses, followed. "Why cause us so much trouble? Why? We have to search for you in our mountains. You make cheap everything nature created for us. The trees cry when they see you; the rocks hide. You people were told when you visited us that you could not enter our mountains where we hold our sacred church. It is closed to you. Forever closed."

Some of the tired hippies derisively rolled their eyes. They could predict there was going to be a brace of speeches, strong speeches by Indians who had a tradition of giving literary orations. It was going to be a long ordeal.

"Wait a second, fella," one of the condemned broke in, "just hold your horses. With due respect, that ain't right. We like the mountains, too. They're also our friends. It's natural for us to want to enjoy them. God made the rivers, valleys, mountains to be used and loved by every person. You don't own the mountain!" His large bushy head fell on his plump chest, as if his speech had squeezed all the air out of him.

To the hippies, he had well represented their side. They rallied their spirits. Their philosophy had been explained. The cry of "you don't own the mountain" gave the hippies some hope of enduring their incarceration. Supportive phrases sprinkled the room: "yeah, man," "right on," "you can say that again."

The litany continued. A young Indian scarred by severe acne stood up, speaking defiantly. "No, we do not own the mountain, but we are the guardians of the mountain, its keepers. We are, not you. It is a sacred trust. Our ancestors were born from this mountain. They are what you call gods and we call kachinas. We were given the responsibility of keeping it clean and pure and we were told to hold our ceremonies there. It is only for us. Not for you. You did not have our permission to stay on the mountain, and we asked you to leave and not return. You waited until night came and with bad thoughts went into our Pueblo and then the mountain. We did not know until the next morning, when we found your evil tracks. We feel sorry for our stream and the flowers who had to see you-and for our unhappy mountain. You lock yourself in our spiritual home. Yes, you wash your dirty underpants in our river. You cut down our trees and leave the wood to rot. You scare the animals and aim guns at them. They hate you, too. You have trespassed on our hearts," and he quickly sat down.

Next, a tall, scrawny man growled in response, "But you folks don't set the rules, whoever you think you are. What do you mean the sacred trust? Who are these gods and kachinas? We are equal to you or anyone. Shit, nobody controls the mountain. The mountains, sky and clouds are for everyone. How can anyone or any group own the mountain? It's not right; it's what's wrong with the country. Everyone wants to be a big capitalist, owning and devouring every item on earth and leaving nothing for just plain people. 'It's mine,' they say, 'all mine.' If you take the mountain away from us we'll have nothing. No individual or organization owns nature. We are the same children of nature you are."

Although the hippies felt their speakers had scored points, they didn't know what could be in store for them-a fight brewing, a trial, going to jail in the Pueblo? Nothing looked good. In spite of their efforts, their opponents seemed to be gathering strength.

A huge brawny man, far bigger than the average native, sprang to his feet, fuming with impatience. "You speak of capitalists who do what they want when they want and destroy what they touch. That is you–that is what you do. You are like maggots who eat out the heart of everything good. Do you have to destroy all our sacred places, our religion, our ceremonies, our Indian values, so that we have nothing left and run around lost, like you people? Our religion is rooted in our mountain. If we don't save the mountain, we people cannot survive. And we do intend to survive. It is your values or ours. And for us our values are not open to debate. We will protect the mountain! Do you get my message?" And he waited there, glaring.

Immediately the other Indian elder stood up and joined in. "You think you can do what you want–get an idea and do it. Go anywhere and dump your garbage and make everything ugly, even if others have rights to the land and you have nothing to do with it. You think you are always right and you listen to no one else. If you harm people, you do not care. You are for you. Nothing else. No, you invaders do not get the message; you never will. Maybe there is only one way for us to handle you."

He stepped forward, and in an instant everybody was on his feet. Apprehensive that fighting could erupt, each side, Indian and hippie, instinctively grabbed each other, holding on tight like a vise in order to prevent any sudden explosion of blows. It was a gesture of restraint. At that moment, all the figures formed a solid frieze.

At that precise instant the door to the room swung open. A rotund woman of about forty peered in.

"Octavio," she said somewhat brusquely, with a question lingering in her tone, "why are you standing there looking so stupid? Are you drunk? What are all these men doing standing dumb like animals? We need you home."

Octavio adjusted his glasses with one hand, turned to his wife and answered, "We are busy right now; we should be through soon."

She stood there, waiting, not trusting anyone.

Then one Indian laughed and withdrew his grip from the human mass. Another Indian also removed his and gave vent to a gusty, sturdy fart.

The rest of the Indians burst out with laughter and they, too, relaxed their stance and let go their hold on one another. To the hippies it was amazing how everyone calmed down. They were freed from impending disaster, standing clear and unattached from the phalanx of Indians. The tension emptied from the room.

Then an Indian yelled, "You better leave now. Now! Be quick or you might not have another chance to get out of here alive."

The hippies were glad to comply, happy to exit unscathed. They ran from the room into the descending night, and considered themselves lucky. In spite of their immense relief in escaping, they could not deny the pull of the mountain.

QUIET

CLEAN AND WELL DRESSED, CLARENCE attended classes in a little town where more than half the pupils were Hispanic. The bus took him to school, and during the seven-mile ride he spoke to no one. He just half-existed. The same bus delivered him back to his dirt driveway where he walked to his small, nondescript adobe house. Each school day, between going and coming, nothing particular happened to him. He remained his pleasant-looking self. He didn't get into trouble, he didn't play hooky. He attended his classes and quietly listened to his teachers. But nothing was added to his day's experience, no knowledge or special feelings. From school bus to school bus he barely changed.

His mother, Sophie, claimed that his languor was due to fragile health, and indeed, Clarence took sick rather frequently with colds and sore throats and was kept home for days at a time to recover. In this condition, Sophie considered him too tender and sensitive to do his homework and his father agreed. "He's a sick boy," his mother was fond of saying, "but he's a good boy." When Clarence returned to school, he was always behind, so he figured it didn't matter whether or not he applied himself. High school was turning out to be an endless chore.

Back when he was only eight years old, Clarence tried to walk to school to avoid his schoolmates, who taunted him for being dumb. En route he was caught by his parents. Overwhelmed by the hysterical insistence of his mother, to whom following the rules was important, his father erupted and violently turned on the boy. Clarence received a severe thrashing. It seemed to him that from then on, whatever happened, he would always be under his parents' control.

Sophie had married Sam after she had gotten pregnant with Clarence. Short, dumpy and slow-witted, none of her Hispanic relatives had dreamed of her being attractive enough to marry, let alone to a drifter from the Midwest who wasn't even Spanish, and who, as an outsider, didn't know the mores of the region. He just got excited in bed with Sophie. As soon as the result of this misdirected foray became apparent, Sam married her. Not withstanding how critically Sophie's family regarded her and her odd gringo husband, Sophie celebrated every moment of her relationship with Sam, and the birth of Clarence was a joyous validation of her womanhood.

There was more to Sam than a random glance would discern. In his forties, large-framed with gray hair intruding on light brown, he had been a jack of many trades. As a boy, he liked to play the oboe and had won a prize in some local music competition, but he then became listless and let his music drop. At fifteen he ran away and apprenticed as a carpenter and later fell into the construction trade. Stable and working steady hours, he married an older woman who conducted a successful beauty salon (not that he thought of her as any kind of beauty). She ran a good home, organized and tidy, and at the end of every month they went through the ritual of adding up their earnings and jointly depositing them at the bank. Afterward, they got drunk.

But as his affairs went smoothly along, Sam became nervous and jumpy because the instability which he craved in his life no longer existed. He began to drink too much rum. One day he didn't return from work to their brand new apartment but instead jumped on a train and headed west. He left everything he owned with his wife, including all the fine, neat pictures holding up the pink plaster walls. He supposed she managed a divorce. The army came next. He enlisted and served out the end of World War II as a cook stationed in one of the Admiralty Islands in the South Seas. He recalled pulpy coconuts and spotless beaches.

Finally he filtered into Sophie's small hometown, which he adopted. A vagrant, he stayed at the Indian pueblo with an Indian couple for a few months, until he met Sophie at a community dance. He was all liquored up and felt horny, and Sophie was so friendly and obliging that he closed his eyes and let himself go. Instantly he owned a family.

Nor was it all bad for Sam. Sophie was a decent wife who cooked credible meals and cleaned the house vigorously. She chattered endlessly, and brought her aunts, including a chosen wealthy one, over to chat in even more voluble tones. Sam vacated the house to sneak a gulp of whiskey from one of the bottles he had cached in the garage. In this way Sam ignored it all. He had purchased a strip of land for a pittance and built a narrow house to fit on it.

He and his docile, puzzled son watched their lives sputter in the alien Spanish, family-oriented lifestyle. The tradition here was that the man ruled (which Sam liked), and he decided to rule completely. Sophie needed organization and a point to revolve around and he furnished these. Plus, he innately felt his wife and her simple black-eyed, black-haired, Mexican relations were backward and weak and knew nothing about the world. He had been abroad in the army, had been tattooed by a primitive native and had lived in a slicked-up apartment in Indianapolis. "These Mexicans, they don't know nuttin," he would tell his son. He wished his son would be more adventurous and blamed this failure on his wife's cluttered behavior and anemic background. She was like a mouse peeping out of her mouse hole, sometimes accompanied by her other peeping mice relations. Even worse, she couldn't drive.

However, the boy was a different matter. Sam could at least train him for some sort of profession, although he barely had one himself. At this point he restored antique furniture and built chairs. He could build a truly durable handmade chair, almost indestructible, and in this age that was no small feat. He even thought of having someone help him write a book on handcrafting indomitable chairs, with which he calculated he could make a fortune similar to that of the inventor of the hairpin. His son should learn the secrets he knew. Sam taught and the boy learned slowly. It was apparent that he did everything slowly, but he did grasp his father's basic instructions. "To make chairs," Sam lectured, "you have to know the technique of joinery." And tentatively Clarence began to absorb his father's trade as a joiner.

Sophie indulged her son, exhibiting him as a paragon of virtues. "A good boy with good thoughts," she boasted. To Clarence the family represented an extended chorus of his mother. It was easy for him to perfectly comply with their whims and entreaties. He could not be ruffled. He even managed to be totally expressionless while inwardly mortified as he told his parents how his high school classmates had cleaned out his lunch box and slipped a big cucumber into it. It was covered with hide and painted to resemble a raw-looking penis.

Clarence failed the second semester of his senior year in high school. He doggedly took the classes over and was happy to hear that he was finally scheduled to graduate. Sam decided to speak to him alone now or he figured it would be too late.

"Clarence, you're kinda different. You don't go with any girls. I've never seen you with a girl. You don't bring home any friends from school to play with. You just stay by yourself. That's not normal. I guess school's no good for you. Funny, I liked school. Even so, you've been a great son, and I expect you'll go on being good and take care of us until your poor parents go off yonder," and Sam waved his hand upward.

"I'm glad school's about over. I learned more from you."

"Me? I ain't done no good, but I couldn't help it. But something's happened. I've just had a feeling for religion come over me, and it's time you and me joined God's Church. We have to wear ties and coats every Sunday. Maybe I can stop drinking that way. You know, I like to take a nip once in a while. Shouldn't do it. Oh, I used to do lots more like that. You wouldn't know. You don't do nuttin. But God's Church can help us. It's gonna tell us when our sins pile up in a heap and anger God so much that he's gonna blot out the world with darkness–and rid the world of all sinners."

They went to a born-again church, father and son. The Catholic wife stayed home and wondered why her husband was so stern in the wrong way. To her, this end-of-the-world business was nonsense.

The day after graduation, the gaggle of aunts and assorted other relatives came to the house to honor Clarence. They seated him in the middle of the couch and surrounded him with questions.

"What do you want to do now?" one aunt asked.

"College? Is that it? You want more school?" his rich aunt inquired.

"What about visiting my cousin who's living in Macon, Georgia? She has a boy your age. It would be good for you to play with someone your own age. Do you good," a cousin affirmed.

Clarence answered his interrogators simply. "I want to stay home. I don't want to go anywhere. I don't like any of the things you people said."

And that settled all matters pertaining to Clarence's immediate future. He was now at peace. He aided his father in joining chairs, helped his mother serve dinner, washed the dishes and dutifully listened to his father repeat how the family could be stronger by obeying God's church and his mother maintain how the family could be stronger by having more family gatherings. In between, he tried to add to his collection of agate marbles (tiger eyes were the best) and old square nails that he found in discarded pieces of antique furniture.

Gradually his parents grew old and his aunts began to slip away. One day his father stated that, as of this moment, he had joined his last chair and consequently was now retired. His mother suffered several severe backaches and stayed in bed much of the time. Hence Clarence joined chairs and scrubbed floors. He had learned to drive his father's Travelall and, taking his father with him, he delivered the finished chairs to clients, bought groceries cheap from a small, family grocery store and attended church every Sunday morning and sometimes on special days.

The rich aunt's husband died and promptly afterwards the rich aunt followed. Clarence and Sophie inherited two hundred thousand dollars worth of land and a small sum of cash. Sophie pointed out to Clarence that, because he paid special attention to his affluent aunt, she put him in her will. Sam hid the cash under the floorboards. Then with his son he cleared the fields of the newly acquired land and planted alfalfa, beans, corn and melons. Continually, other family members died, until hardly anyone came to see them. Occasionally one of the members of Sam's church arrived, bringing a Bible and pronouncing some new impending doom that would certainly take place. He stroked Clarence's head and blessed him for spending his life taking care of his parents.

Every once in a while Sam would speak disconnectedly about how he saw the islanders almost naked on their sunny islands and how, as soon as he came back to the States, he had a pornographic tattoo changed into a lover's heart with an arrow through it. Then he would turn to his dearest subject and dwell on his vengeful God.

Sophie took on a new tact and would plaintively insist that Clarence should leave both of them and go out into the world and find what was outside for him–some new faces or ideas, because nothing happened in this place. As soon as she spoke, tears oozed forth and she would catch herself, for she realized that it was she who tied her son down to the gleaming floorboards underneath him. It was no use.

Sam and Sophie practically died on top of each other, one day apart. One funeral was ordered for them, managed by the Catholic church. Scarcely a person was left to attend, only two weary church members and an old Pueblo Indian who used to help Sophie clean house.

Clarence had a store of groceries on hand, and the night of the funeral he boiled potatoes. He ate measuredly on the kitchen table where the family had taken food. He fiddled with the matched pair of cheap carnival-ware salt and pepper shakers and then unexpectedly decided that he didn't want dinner mats. He preferred the warm, dark wood shining under his plate. He was sure his parents wouldn't mind. He thought it best to pull down the blinds. A thorough cleaning of the house was in order. His mother hadn't been physically able to perform that duty for nearly two years. Outside, he went to the workshop in the garage and lit a fire. His father always had huge stacks of wood scattered around the yard. Warm and comfortable, he joined chairs for an order he had. His father had been too slow. In his bedroom he played migs. Every time he took aim with his best tiger-eye agate shooter and propelled it with some force into the target marble, he said "pow," reveling in the spectacle of the marbles colliding into each other. "Pow, pow!" He was in bed at nine, the traditional bedtime for him and his parents, but he couldn't sleep. So what. They weren't around.

He and the morning popped up early, this time before the alarm clock chattered away like his mother. He had been long awake, guessing whether the alarm clock would still do its job or just peacefully rest and do nothing. He didn't have to do anything. But he arose and chose a shirt to put on that he hadn't worn for some time, although he always had in mind to rotate it along with his other shirts. He was glad he discovered it because he wasn't using, and thus was wasting, it. Breakfast on the naked wood of the table was delightfully different. He put jam on his toast and began to tinker with the toaster. Only he could consistently make it work. His father couldn't, although he refused to have it fixed.

He remembered that the flowers needed to be watered, even the cactus once in awhile. One day he would have to buy groceries, and sooner or later, in fact, soon, he should deliver the chairs he had finished and get paid. It was true that he could have used Sam when he harvested their crops but he really didn't need him. He had no problems. There was plenty of money in the house, the telephone worked, although nobody would call, and the mail would be deposited in the mailbox. He didn't figure there would be much mail coming. He knew how to use the bank if he needed to. Everything was in its place–orderly. Nothing could surprise him or upset him. A quilt of quiet spread its weight over the house. Just quiet.

His parents had planned his future well.

REHEARSAL

THE TRYOUTS FOR THE OLD IRISH play were held under bleak conditions. The weather was gray and the interior of the building for the auditions was dark and somber. In this town of five thousand survivors, though, the citizens were lucky to have a theater at all. Most communities of that size had none. Those who came to the casting session were all recent arrivals from other climes-Chicago, Louisiana, New York-who were attracted to living under a huge mountain in the high desert, where it snowed in the winter and heated up in the summer.

As director, he had little to choose from. He had a candidate to play the crafty king (a local lawyer), one for the handsome prince (a chunky jeweler), and one for the ravishing, young queen. She was around twenty-five, theatrically well trained, with unruly black hair and immaculate white skin. She was sultry Irish, southern, with lots of pretty little bones slightly over-fleshed. He would have preferred someone younger, until he was talked out of this by his assistant director, who said he was crazy if he didn't take at least one professional actor.

He wondered if it would turn out to be good advice. It was late on a Sunday afternoon when he picked his cast, including an Irishman as Fergus, a powerful friend of the play's king, and he scheduled rehearsals for every week night. As he left, his assistant, Amelia, whispered, "You did it right. Never take youth over experience. She can really act–better than I can." Coming from Amelia, who lusted to act in any major part and in any available play, that was good to hear.

His cast congregated at the town auditorium in the late dusk of a cool autumn. They waited at the iron front door while he unlocked it. They went through the foyer and into the theater, passing rows of empty seats, and then they stepped up to the stage itself. There they gathered some chairs, sat down in a circle and with the lights on, faced the ghosts of past audiences. The invisible assembly looked back upon them as if they were a question mark, undeveloped and unrealized, and indeed, he figured they were just that, lost shades that had not yet emerged into the light of day. He would illuminate them.

"John Synge wrote *Dierdre of the Sorrows*, based on an ancient Celtic legend, and he died in 1909, not having quite finished the play. He cast his lover, an Irish actress, as Dierdre, and she starred in the first performance after his painful death. Death stalks throughout this play. We are talking about the death of a queen, the shattering of her royal lover, the demise of a king, and the mythical death of Ireland before the time of Christ." He paused. "Ash, you play Dierdre. Who is she?"

Ash stroked her black hair and replied, "She's pretty much an enigma, but she did her thing."

"What motivated her?"

"Passion," she said, "pure passion. She lived for love with no limits. Like a wild animal."

"But she turned her back on that to go live with the king and royalty."

"Remember the prophecy foretold," Earl broke in, "that Dierdre was to marry me, the king, or Ireland would burn to the ground. Even in her rush to escape with the prince to the woods for seven years, she could never get rid of her impending doom."

He was pleased. A good discussion was brewing. He thought that the man was well cast as the king-in his bearded forties, with a deep, forceful voice.

He answered. "Perhaps. But Dierdre really didn't want to live with an old wrinkled despot. So why did she renounce living blissfully in the woods for you and your throne?"

Ash spoke: "Because she could see that her ideal union with the prince had peaked. She couldn't bear to live for anything less than perfection."

"More to the point," the prince joined in, "I misled her by an offhand remark. It was my fault. She overheard some crap I said to Fergus and thought my love was dying out, which wasn't so. She was wrong."

"She couldn't stand any doubt," Ash said. "It had to be all-out love."

"A description of an existentialist," Fergus chimed in. "She lives just from moment to moment."

He broke it up. "Rehearsal is over," he said. He had them in his hand.

He and Ash left the auditorium together, and he asked her if she would like to go some place where they could talk. She appealed to him not only as an actress with unerring dramatic instincts but also as a woman. In his forties, he was conscious of their age difference. In her role-playing a distinct sensual quality revealed itself. Ardent on the stage, he imagined she might be equally ardent offstage. They went to a dive that stayed open late. They talked but not about anything in particular. Less radiant now, she complained that her job wasn't going well and that her mother in Kansas was ill. She was working as a waitress. She wanted to be an actress, to do serious acting. In a small Louisiana college she had been in some plays and her professor liked her acting. She was the only one he knew who spoke faultless English with a southern drawl. As a director, he was a little surprised that she didn't have more background than this, but she was quick to learn. He tried to impress her with dabs of arcane knowledge. He did mention that he had an estranged wife. She tried to pay for french fries and tea, but she didn't have the money, so he paid and they parted.

He looked over the empty symmetry of seats, no longer remote to him but just waiting to be occupied.

Ash was different on stage; she shone like amber, flaws and all. He pointed at her. "This girl has been socked away in a cottage and raised by an old nurse until she's mature and has to marry the king. He's her guardian and her jailer. How does she feel about this?"

The actress shrank between her shoulder blades. "She really can't stand him. She's frightened to marry him and yet, because of the prophecy, she's afraid not to be his queen."

Earl said, "The old man has wattles. He's lonely. He's got a big gut. At seventeen, he's afraid she'll be snagged. He can't wait to get his hands on her."

"But what about Dierdre?" the director said. "She sees the prince and his brothers from the cottage window. Ash, explain her thoughts."

"I think he is the most gorgeous young man in this land of green. He's the greenest god I ever saw. I saw him hunting in the woods. I wished I could have been the deer."

The prince beamed, clearly flattered. "I tried to warn you," he raised his hands in futility. "The prophecy. The curse. Ireland in flames and all that jazz. You just teased me straight to hell and snared me."

Suddenly, his director's eye detected movement in the back of the theater. An audience of one was out there. He recognized one of Ash's friends, a young woman whom he had once met.

Ash spoke: "Yes, but you, pinhead, were my only way out. And you were really beautiful. But so conservative. I had to stoke your stove for sure. I won."

"Not long enough," the prince sulked. "The king got you to go back to the throne."

"But we did have seven happy years," she smiled, "a lifetime. Better to have that than a long stay on earth writhing in boredom."

"The king betrayed me, too," Fergus spoke. "He gave his pledge to me that the lovers would be safe, and they believed me."

"Let's go home," said Earl. "I'm tired. All this doom can wait until tomorrow."

Again he and Ash joined company, and he chose a place where nobody would know him. He wanted to proceed carefully. Ash was vague, almost blurry. She had quit her waitress job and was planning to move in with a friend. Theater, not her personal life, was the bond between them. He mentioned that he had plans for her in his next opus. He told her that she was an accomplished actress with ability. Pleased, she thanked him and held his hand, but when he kissed her, she didn't react. Disappointed, he climbed into his car and left.

At the next rehearsal (she was always on time), she had the same amber smile but not especially for him. Yet she was still an evening flower blooming in the vacant auditorium.

He remarked, "At the end the lovers die apart. Why can't they unite in death?"

"Because doubt poisoned their love," said Ash, "and under the stress of their capture by the king, they were at cross-purposes with each other. She, solely thinking of his love for her, but he, the prince, of the whole disaster–his demise and his brothers' and the destruction of his country."

"The king sowed conflict between the lovers," Earl announced. "The prince is fighting for his life while Dierdre is the royal pet and future bride. Their stakes are not the same. Caught between his own sealed fate and her open destiny, the prince breaks down, believing Dierdre has brought about his death. He dies an embittered man."

"Yes, damn right, but I didn't surrender. Hell, no. I died fighting. No way I'd get down begging on bended knee to that old goat."

His cast was caught up in the make-believe; the director knew he had succeeded.

"Ash," he asked, "why in the end did Dierdre stab herself?"

"Because she was the cause of the prince's death. Life was over for her. She could only be a drudge for the king, that wonderful man," Ash laughed.

"But," he insisted, "all the king had to do to maintain a peaceful and prosperous reign was to temporarily accept the relationship of the lovers, and then later take Dierdre for himself. Why did he refuse? He was obviously obsessed with Dierdre."

"Yes," Earl agreed, "you are right. I did push events. But I did not think there would be consequences. I thought that once I had the prince eliminated and had Dierdre solely as my love and queen, I would be victor. Ireland then could not be destroyed. I did not foresee her taking her life. That act of hers is what broke me. Crushed me."

Fergus countered: "Because of Dierdre's death, I destroyed Ireland by fire. With my armies I fulfilled the prophecy because you broke your word first to me and then to the lovers. You betrayed them and brought yourself down to a life of empty futility."

Applause came from the back of the theater. Ash's friend and Amelia were loudly clapping their hands.

"You guys are good," Amelia declared. "It sounds like it's part of the play. Great!"

This time he did not take Ash out to eat. He stayed in the car with her and talked. He told her he could develop her into a superb actress, and that he had the means to promote her. His antique business was successful. By working together they would become lovers. He called her Dierdre by mistake and apologized. He didn't want them to become doomed lovers. He kissed her deeply and she became inert, limp, kissing him with no personal involvement. He put his hand under her white linen blouse and felt her uncovered breast. She moved slightly and said they should continue at her house. He agreed and they rode in silence through the streets.

She lived in a cheap apartment with few virtues, except that it was across the street from a park. She waited a minute before getting out of the car. In trying to kiss her he clumsily honked the horn. She wanted to know if he didn't think that tomorrow was a better time for them; she was exhausted. He said no, and they got out. After walking up a few steps, she hesitated. He told her to go on. She turned the knob of the door and opened it.

Before them, sitting on the couch, scantily dressed in a nightgown, was the woman from the audience. She rose, came over and kissed Ash with fervor. Ash in turn kissed her friend passionately, embracing her around the waist and pulling her tight against herself. Impervious to his presence, they stared into each other's eyes. Ash still wore her lovely smile, but now it was infused with ardor.

He stepped back, reflecting that one pair of ill-fated lovers in the play was enough.

THIRD WORLD ENCOUNTER

DONALD W. THORNBURG WALKED INTO the Indian Pueblo casually and looked around furtively. He glanced at its two three-story adobe buildings, separated by a percolating river and dominated by a mesmerizing mountain. It reminded him of a blowup of a museum diorama of some primitive village.

He slipped through the shabby surroundings of this third world realm, avoiding attention. He carried his weighty purpose within him as if hidden in a secret inner pocket. He was in fine spirits, the bearer of good news in a job he performed cleanly and efficiently. As a thirty-four year-old unmarried business management graduate with honors, he supported the government philosophy of helping impoverished, indigenous peoples provide for themselves. In point, the Pueblo was eligible for aid because of its similarity to non-industrialized countries whose natives live close to the land in dwellings made from local materials. Because of its identity with certain Latin American and African territories using adobe in home construction, the Pueblo was given a high classification to receive a grant. In fact, Donald had just heard from Washington that a sizable disbursement of funds had been extended to the Pueblo for general improvements. He was appointed the singular agent to hand deliver the message.

Humming the theme to Elgar's regal and lengthy *Pomp and Circumstance*, Donald supplied his own words, in the form of his elongated full name, to the dignified and stately processional. He sang it repeatedly and slowly, in measured cadence, to fit perfectly the rhythm: "Donald W. Thornburg, Donald W. Thornburg." Savoring his name, he marched deliberately through the music and approached the chief's old house.

Telesforo Duran, swinging his sparse gray ponytail, intercepted Donald at the screen door before he could enter and motioned him, with a flick of the hand, to sit down on a weathered bench lining the wall on one side of the doorway. The younger man obeyed and settled against the comfortable adobe wall.

"Telesforo," Donald droned, "I have come to bring you a communication from the government. Do you understand?"

He wondered why the stocky, respected elder was addressed with a common Spanish name instead of an Indian title. Probably he had one but wouldn't let it be known to outsiders. Donald noticed, however, the traditional faded cotton trade blanket wrapped around Telesforo's store-bought clothes. Telesforo, in turn, focused his wearied eyes beyond the busy Government Man who so frequently made rounds inspecting the place. What he did know about the person next to him was that his closely cropped hair, whistle-clean shave and shiny new clothes conformed to his tight attitude. He was either eager and overly friendly or cautious and manipulating, or an uneasy mix of both, and consequently to Telesforo he was of little substance. The two men stared out at the broad, dirt-strewn plaza rimmed by boxy adobe houses.

The Indian responded after a considerable lapse of time. "You said you talk to the government? What does government say to us?"

"I am glad you asked that question." Donald quickly but measuredly grinned. "Do you remember we talked about the financial aid the government was considering giving to the Pueblo? Well, the government has made that decision and you are awarded the grant. It's yours."

Telesforo nodded. Try as he may, what he could not forget about this man was that during every visit he talked about money, help and good times for the Pueblo. "I remember," Telesforo mumbled.

"I'm proud of you. Well, we, I mean the government in Washington does not wish to be thanked or anything like that, but we sure think you can use the money to fix up the Pueblo."

"Our people thank you. You give us news, but we're happy with our Pueblo. We keep it fine," the elder stated.

"You are a happy people by nature, yet I think you deserve to be happier and live better," the outsider shrugged.

"Uh-huh. We like our ways and this place has been a good home for us. We know that. We get along fine. You no worry."

"Still, there is room for improvement for everyone. Even me," Donald poked himself and fizzled a smile. "The government is offering you a grant for which you qualified, and we believe you should take advantage of it. Think of all those others in need that the government has passed over in selecting the Pueblo," he said pompously. "Some might say you are lucky to be chosen."

"This grant, what does it mean to the Pueblo?"

"What does it mean?" the visitor blurted. "As I said before, it means that the government is willing to hand you $250,000 to clean up your village and to make it spic-and-span and attractive. A good deal for everybody. Absolutely."

"This grant you say does a strange thing. How does the grant do spic-span and make things better? Why?"

"Why?" the government man tried to muffle his irritation. "Because it provides work for your people. Tearing down the rotten and crumbling buildings and removing all the rubble and debris will give them something to do. It's for a good cause. This place is a safety hazard. Then you build new, decent houses that will look nice. You will be happy with them. Not that we don't have our slums, too," he said condescendingly, "but your home will be like new and the Pueblo will be clean and pretty."

"We think this place here is already pretty for us and we don't want clean. Buildings always are this way and stand up pretty good. Old ones sometimes get tired and fall down. Some get fixed up. Like we do. We want it that way."

"But certainly you want this town-and pardon me, it is a small town-to be sanitary so you and your children can be healthy. Look around! This whole area is just dirt and dust. And what about the outhouses? Scads of them. How can you tolerate them and the dirt?"

"No one dies from dirt. Dirt is good. You always speak bad of dirt. If we don't drink whiskey we live a long life. Your government gives us one hospital if we get sick. Okay, we have that. We don't need sanitary."

"Listen here! We are offering you a quarter of a million dollars to improve your community and make it livable, so you can be proud of it. The money has already been allocated for this project, so it's yours. Understand? It's like the money is in the bank. You own it."

Telesforo Duran, deliberately calculating its effect on him, retreated to silence, rooted in his boots, minus their heels following Pueblo Indian custom, and retrenched his thoughts. Finally his words tumbled with the solemnity of gravestones. "No, we say. No! We don't want better. What you say is better is no better for us. We like what we have. You stay where you are. We stay on this ground, good for our feet. Ground maybe not clean like you want but we don't care. We tell you no. You keep grant. Grant is yours. Now you talk no more of this. Be quiet."

"But in the name of humanity you have to accept the grant; it belongs to you. How can you be so illogical?" And with smoldering frustration Donald W. Thornburg grabbed the Indian by the shoulders and shook him with rough, jerky movements. "You simply must not refuse our grant; you have to accept it," and he shook his victim harder. "It is budgeted in our account and financially paid for by the sweat of the American taxpayer. It's in the computer. I will not allow you to say no. If you never change, you will become stagnant," and suddenly aware of his actions, he loosened his hold on the man.

"I must go now and feed pigs; you must go, too. You should not place your hands on my shoulder. They are heavy. Leave me alone. Now! You get excited. Government gets crazy idea and runs around like fool. Too bad! You do dumb things. Now you go and I go. Good-bye," and Telesforo walked away.

Donald W. Thornburg traced the departing man as he headed across the plaza to the pig corrals, and he sighed for lost opportunity, endless questions, difficult explanations and extra paperwork.

THE BAVARIAN CAPER

I DON'T REALLY KNOW MOST OF THE people where I live. Recently, newcomers seem to come here to get rid of what originally ailed them. All they do is dump their past on new ground-my little Southwest town, framed against the mountains, but unfortunately not people-proof.

I make a certain distinction about myself when I claim I am not one of these newcomers, because I had long ago planned to live in Myopia and had researched the place beforehand. Until now only a few people resided here in unbounded space where they kept to themselves and tried to be forgotten. My wife and I decided that such a home would ideally suit us. After our move, we found that the prevailing old-timers had ossified on the land, turning starched and crusty, their features sharply landscaped like the terrain itself. They were likable and easy to mingle with since they considered the newly arrived, such as us, rare and news in itself.

But nothing stayed still. Within a few years, when the outsiders gradually began to equal the insiders of the town, they began to stick out. The latest crop indelibly altered the town's complexion. They brought wealth, gloss and little else. These newcomers scarcely had contact with, not to say feeling for, the folks in general who were down-on-their-luck and the Hispanics in particular, many of whom held marginal and uncertain jobs.

One of my pals was a furniture restorer, Evaristo Esquibel, although we called him Hector, even though no one had the slightest notion why. Perhaps there was no way to nickname Evaristo and Hector was much simpler. In his early thirties, Hector recently married his attractive high school sweetheart. He came into my life because I sold antique furniture and often used him as a restorer. He was good with wood; in fact, he was heard to say "the wood is good." He could transfigure a tired, rickety, splintery, old, dried-up, Hispanic *trastero* or *cajon* into a beautifully restored cabinet or chest, glistening with soft luster. Hector told me of a couple who had slipped into the community unobtrusively six months ago and had employed him to massage their pieces of antique furniture on a regular weekly basis. He was paid to be their custodian, a great deal. He had mentioned me and my house of old collectibles to them, and that I was known as the local collector of fine arts.

I was having dinner at home with some guests when the woman who employed Hector arrived at my front door, peered through the window and asked to see the adobe rooms inside, if only for a moment, so as not to disturb the small gathering. I had to disappoint her, as I was just about to eat a slice of one year-old mutton my neighbor had killed and I didn't want the beast to get any older. It was simply not a good time. Politely, she said she understood and perhaps another time would do.

That other time took place in reverse when Hector told me that my wife and I were invited to have dinner with him and Isabel at the house of his patrons and friends. In order to accommodate Hector, my wife Roses (sometimes called Rose) and I accepted. Driving en route, Hector gave us a verbal dossier on our hosts. Names: Gertrude and Ray Campion; Origin: Germany for Gertrude and Oklahoma for Ray. Hector explained that Ray was Gertrude's second husband.

As we started down the paved pathway to an imposing adobe house, Gertrude stepped out to greet us. I was particularly taken by her face, still quite beautiful even at her age, which I guessed to be in the late sixties. She graciously escorted us to the door, stopped us and asked if we would take off our shoes.

"I realize you are a collector, a collector of fine furniture," she said. "I looked into your home for a second when I dropped by and saw some Biedemier items, excellent examples. When you walk into my house you will see similar pieces, and removing your shoes before you enter shows a certain sense of dedication. Besides, I don't want you to scuff the waxed floors. I know you will understand."

We dutifully removed our shoes and stacked them into little piles.

She addressed me. "When I enter your house I will do the same."

We clustered into a small hallway that led into an enormous room, a world of the spectacular. Huge Bavarian painted chests, one dated 1722 and another 1802, were decorated with colorful floral designs. There were several painted cabinets, benches and matched chairs (twelve of them around a large, venerable table, glowing with a delicious patina). Beckoning at my left was a wooden mangle with a luster-rubbed handle fashioned in the shape of a wondrous lion, who looked over the end of the board with four depictions of German life and a date inscribed 1726. To the right I caught pictures of rural scenes painted on reverse glass, sparkling fresh and bright. In the corner was an imposing early standing clock in working order. It was easy to be awed by superb taste. I stared so hard my eyeballs hurt. Then I let out a sigh of wonderment, turned in a circle and produced a little dance for all to see. Gertrude sent me a look of fervent gratitude.

"You know!" she trembled. "You really know. You're the only one who would respond. In the whole town I sensed you alone would understand. I could tell by your house how you would react to mine."

"Bavarian folk art," I cried, "a perfect little museum, as good as any German provincial museum. And right here? Unbelievable! It's a marvelous dream."

"I lived in a castle in Bavaria and like you I became a collector," she said.

At that moment a graying, gentle-looking man, somewhere in his sixties and casually dressed, walked in and offered me his hand, which I shook.

"I'm Ray, Gertrude's husband, and I guess you're Cecil and Roses. Good to see you, Hector, Isabel. Excuse my wife's excitement. She hasn't seen anybody here who has her same interests and knows what these things are."

Ignoring him, Gertrude broke in, clearly agitated. "Pay no attention. What's important is that you are here-that you have come to this haven to share it with me-that you are aware."

Ray stepped backward. "It's nice to have compatible company, but you don't want to get too excited. It's not good for you. I'm making barbecue ribs on the grill in the patio. In ten minutes dinner will be ready."

Hector and Isabel offered to help.

Rejecting what she deemed unnecessary concerns, Gertrude sharply steered me and Roses further into the room. "Never mind Ray," she countered. "We will continue," and looked knowingly at Roses and me.

Now concentrating fully on Gertrude, I realized that I liked looking at her. Her once light brown hair was now melanged with a dusky gray and curled delicately around her neck, further enhancing her classically modeled nose, a lush mouth and graceful chin. She was dressed attractively in a beige skirt and an exquisite heather-green blouse with a small, dainty neckline. On her blouse perched an almost ephemeral pin of costume jewelry, which I suspected was made by a goldsmith so seasoned that he disdainfully replaced the common gold in favor of a network of secret stones from the earth, which he spun into a broach. She was a princess, albeit a defrocked one, living in a tucked away town with her husband, who was a nice enough guy. On the wall a ceramic plate painted with a mythical animal enticed me to look more closely, if that is possible for one who is glued to art. Early, early, it was, probably fifteenth century Renaissance. "Fabulous!" I was enthralled. She fluttered, then shook her head with appreciation, a deep gesture of fulfillment.

"One of my best," she glowed. "You, of course, would not miss it. Obviously."

Just then Ray appeared from the kitchen wearing a tall white traditional cook's hat and an apron. He paused, then approached us slowly, a frown on his face.

"Calm down," he said to his wife, "I've never seen you so agitated-much too much so. It's not good for you. I'm sure you don't mind," he turned to me, "if she comes with me to help set the table."

Her husband's remarks only served to increase Gertrude's fervor. "Ray, you are interrupting me. Now please serve the dinner."

Resigned, he dropped his head and stood silent, saying nothing for a few seconds.

"All right, all right," he muttered, "but do try to take care of yourself. Please, listen to me, for your own good! Please," and he reentered the kitchen.

Gertrude waited until he disappeared. "He means well, but he doesn't really understand me."

And then I saw what I had guessed I would find. On the wall hung an old black and white photograph of her, taken by a professional photographer. Yes, she had every bit of the commanding elegance I had expected. She was then a muted blond. A fur piece was draped around her neck, with an edge of pearls visible. Even in black and white her eyes looked blue. I glanced at her and her eyes were still blue, only a little faded. It somewhat pleased me that she had once been an extraordinary beauty.

"You," I pointed, "truly a living treasure."

"Once upon a time–1934," she mused, "a lot of time has gone by. Just married in Berlin when everything turned into gold dust and settled around my feet. What a difference it has been."

I was particularly struck with her beauty because I knew about ravishing German film actresses of the past-Lil Dagover, Marlene Dietrich, the early Hedy Lamarr-and Gertrude could have easily qualified.

"There," I indicated, crossing into a small room, "there, those drawings, I know them. They're by Schiele, Egon Schiele. With all his talent he died young. An Austrian genius. How did you manage to own three Schieles?"

Before me was a skinny, muscle-knotted nude, a portrait of two men's heads resting on each other and a self-portrait of the painter, lying down with his organ exposed.

"A remarkable artist," I continued.

"Not quite so remarkable," she interjected. "He gave my husband a bad time."

"Your husband?" I inquired.

"Yes. He was considerably older than me. When he became artistic director for the German museums, he defended Schiele as an artist and tried to include him in the State's national collections. Because of Schiele's erratic and deviant behavior, which the authorities deemed disgusting, my husband had much abuse heaped on him. His critics regarded everything Schiele stood for as being against everything the German State believed in. Since my husband's father was an artist, there were those who said he had an unstable background and was unfit to be an important director. Although he stayed on, the strain he underwent led to his early death."

Ray popped his head into the room and scrutinized his wife. "You all right?" Then he grimaced. "Gertrude, you are about to take off like a balloon and pop! Get a hold of yourself. You're not your normal self. Please excuse her." He looked at me.

Gertrude disregarded him, and he turned back. She faced my wife. "As you were saying, I gather you two are admirers of Egon Schiele."

Roses spoke. "It doesn't matter what kind of man he was. Who cares if Schiele beat his wife or not, or whether he was accepted by his peers. What does count is the fact that his work is great. That's what's meaningful."

"You can say that if you wish," Gertrude burst out, "but my husband suffered from just being associated with him. Schiele was his nemesis. But, of course, you are not involved."

"We are very interested," Roses added, "because it's the artist's work that takes precedence over his personal life. That is why you hang his drawings in this room-because you enjoy them."

"Never mind," Gertrude rejoined. "What my husband still managed to accomplish was a miracle in spite of Schiele and his like." She picked up a memento. "Here is a statue that was given to him from the State. Only five of these were presented to Chiefs of State, men like the founder of the

Volkswagen car and Albert Speer, head of production. My husband received this statue as an award."

I examined it closely and handed it to Roses. The statue had a Christian cross engraved on its breast, but underneath was some other symbol we couldn't decipher because it had been obliterated. But on closer examination, the barely visible outline of a swastika was apparent.

"He was a person of importance," Gertrude emphasized.

"Absolutely amazing," I enthused, "all this incredible art stored in an oasis."

"The creme de la creme," she shuddered, thrilled, "and there was more. I had much more but I couldn't take it all out of the country. There were restrictions, although even at the end the officials were most generous to me."

"The officials were your friends?" I asked.

"Oh, yes. Goebels used to kiss my white gloves and Goering would fly me in his private plane. There was no limit to my rich life there."

For a moment everyone was silent.

The ringing of a bell sounded and Ray, Hector and Isabel filed into the room.

"Dinner is ready. Come and get it," Ray announced. He nodded pointedly at me. "You know you can't eat art."

"Indeed," I replied, "sage words."

"I am not hungry," Gertrude remarked.

Ray quickly took her hand, "Please honor us with your presence just the same," and he firmly escorted her around toward the patio. "Sitting down with us will do you good."

At dinner we talked just to fill out the time. Gertrude said very little and Ray watched her closely. He commented that she had overdone her social duties and was now tired. He also complained that he had been so distracted by his wife's behavior that he hadn't cooked the barbecue enough to achieve a crisp finish. Hector had no complaints; he preferred rare meat, even chicken.

"Yuk," Isabel commented.

I asked if I could have the bones for my dog, but Hector also had a dog. We decided we had to split the bones evenly. I had the first choice and took the biggest bone. Hector groaned and unfairly snatched the next two, and the process resumed until he picked the last bone. The evening dwindled uneventfully, and we thanked the Campions profusely. Ray dutifully asked us to return. Gertrude briefly asserted herself, "Now it is my turn to visit your house." We put our shoes on. Hector and I slapped each other on the back and we went out together.

After I had dropped off the Esquibels, I sighed to my wife, "What a caper! Did you enjoy the party?"

"She must have remarried when she came to the States. But I wonder if he knows? He must know a lot, but does he know everything?"

"She was beautiful," I offered, "a real magnate of beauty."

"Can you follow me?" she flicked. "Do you feel he knows everything?"

"All she wants is to see our collection and for us to recognize her as an art connoisseur. That's the main reason she invited us over. It's sad."

"Impossible. She can never come!" Roses blurted. "Why are you evading me?"

"First answer my question," I pursued. "Did you like the party?"

She paused. "Oh, the dinner was acceptable, and the art objects quite absorbing, but over all, I guess I felt uncomfortable having dinner with a Nazi. Do you think she knows we are Jewish?"

LOST IN THE SAGEBRUSH NOWHERE

I AM SIMPLY A DOG. NO, THE WORD SIMPLY IS NOT right. I am a male Chow dog, around eight years old (my guess), with thick, rust-colored hair. My name is Kahn, based on my mistress' maiden name. I am Chinese-American, since my earliest ancestors some two thousand years ago came from China, and I was born in Santa Fe, New Mexico, USA. I am not ashamed to admit that I am rather handsome, full in the chest, black-tongued (my breed's uniqueness) and endowed with a broad, short snout. My master doesn't groom me, leaving my fur scraggly and full of burrs and stickers. I think I deserve better treatment, although in general I am affectionately treated and well fed. I live in a small Spanish-American village. My home is on a mesa overlooking miles of sagebrush and beneath a high hill. My favorite pastime is chasing rabbits year round, and in the summer I go after chipmunks, too. This is not an easy task. You can imagine all the time that I have devoted to pursuing rabbits every day of every year. But, unfortunately, when you consider that this is my life's work, I've caught very few of them. Sad. Still my years are an eternal flow of never-ending pleasures.

Then it came to be that during the last summer the daughter and son-in-law of my master and mistress visited us and brought with them their little girl, two years old. I liked them, but I do not think the man cared for me. From the beginning he was afraid I would bite his child. He continually scowled at me and I knew he wished me to go away. His girl had inherited the fear of dogs biting her from her father and acted uneasy with me. I was abundantly unwanted. The last day before they left, the man and his daughter entered the house from the outside guest house and somehow I did not hear them. I was taken by surprise. I jumped at them, nipping the girl. In a rage the man ordered me outside, to be locked up in a fenced area. My master reluctantly complied and made me a prisoner. I confess I should not have leaped at them, and I did not mean to harm the child. I could tell the man hated me and would never forget his hatred.

It was winter when I heard from my owners that the family of the little person was again coming to see us. This was most disturbing. My owners discussed for days on end the possibility of sending me to board in a kennel. Both were against making me leave home but did not know how to handle the situation. They were concerned about the reaction of their son-in-law. Consequently, just before the arrival of the visitors, they took me in their car for a long ride.

On a freezing, snowy day I was brought to a boarding house where I smelled dogs, lots of dogs. They were in separate cages, each with a small shelter at one end connected to a long, narrow, concrete runway where the dogs could move about in restricted spaces. I held back. I savored the smell of other dogs, but I didn't wish to be left there alone. My master, realizing that I might escape, put a leash around my neck, but as usual he fumbled with the snap. I tried to jerk free. Then he picked me up and carried me inside the office. Every time he does that, I know by his breathing and awkwardness that I am quite heavy.

Inside, he talked to the kennel owners about letting me remain with them and their dog in their apartment at night and about providing me with a large fenced enclosure to roam in during the day, all for a higher price. They agreed, and he stooped down and kissed me on my head. He foolishly always kisses me. Then he left and drove away.

I regarded the people who were holding me, and they seemed sufficiently pleasant. But I had never stayed away from home before and I was becoming most unhappy. The woman took me inside to her apartment and introduced me to her pet, a Cairn terrier called Amanda-Panda, who slept a lot and yapped a lot and did nothing in between. She rested on a satin pillow in the shape of a heart and was given special biscuits several times a day, while I was fed cheap, store-brand food. Complementing her spoiled ways, she was nicknamed Precious. I found her neither precious nor interesting. Above all, she couldn't have sex. I tried. She certainly couldn't run down a rabbit; in fact, I doubt if she had ever seen one.

That night I slept soundly in a corner of the room, warm and protected from the cold outside. The atmosphere here was all right but boring. At home my owners would scream and laugh at each other, constantly causing my ears to prick up. They would throw me snippets of strange, odd-tasting scraps from the table and talk to me and ask questions, as if I could talk back. Stupid antics. And my master would invariably bend down on his knees and kiss me, even in front of company. Now I was barred from going on my daily outings–crossing the sagebrush on a bright day to the church and over to Bill-the-Painter's house and then down to the river to cool off and finally to the wide bend in the road where my playmates would assemble. These were my haunts, which I personally watered each day. What made me even more homesick was that I dreamed about rabbits, those cottontails, and sometimes the jacks, nibbling on grass and warily looking up, with their noses twitching and their ears straight up and long. Of course I rushed them and they spurted forth every which way, pouring out of the sagebrush, jumping, hopping, springing, dancing around me. Every time I tried to take a bite of one, another would attract my attention, and I never managed to sink my teeth into anything except some rabbit fur. I awoke whimpering and quivering in frustration. I think I had a fever, I was so hot and excited.

In the morning it was snowing heavily. I was let out into the enclosure that didn't have a blade of grass on the ground, even under the snow. My fenced-in compound was larger than the others, roomier, but roomier to do what? To sit blinking in the snow. To do what I have to do. Even after I had released my bodily substances onto the snow and patiently waited an hour, no one let me go inside. The snow bombarded everything. Rabbits wouldn't stand out in the snow like this. They would be inside little wombs in the ground. I decided I didn't want to remain here. At the end of the yard next to the fence I found a small hole which I worked hard to enlarge by digging under the fence. My claws gouged the earth and dirt rapidly flew up and spread itself around, coloring the snow. Soon I created a space where I could slip under the metal mesh. As I gazed at the kennels, I could see the other dogs watching me. They were probably wishing they were in my position. Happily, I was free.

    I ran along the snow-covered road on which I was driven to the kennel. I passed the other dogs, who whined and whimpered as I went by. They were both happy and sorry for me, but I didn't wait to find out why. Reaching another road bordered by a long ridge, I turned away from the kennel into some open sagebrush-covered land, spotted with a few houses. I was satisfied just to run-to be off and away. It was marvelous to stretch my muscles and glide by bushes, taking in the smell of horses, cows and the residue of other strays like myself. But, alas, there were no rabbits. I slid underneath a barbed wire fence and entered a yard that smelled comfortably of my dog friends. I had the misfortune to run into an old venomous goose, standing much taller than I and ruffled with anger. The orbs of her eyes maddened and she lunged at me, stabbing my head with her forceful beak, just missing my eye. I cringed with pain, wheeled around and fled from this feathered disaster, taking some hair off my back as I sped under the barbed wire fence. Looking back, I could see the tyrant still waddling toward me, infuriated, with the snow nestling white on her smooth white back.

    I raced down another narrow road and noticed that a car had turned in behind me. It kept on following me and started to overtake me. This was serious. By this time I was running my fastest and still the car rapidly gained on me. I attempted to swerve out of its way but the snow was banked high on each side of the road. The car pressed at my heels and there were no seconds to lose. My last chance was to steel my head and shoulders together and crash into a wall of snow, churning my legs forward with every ounce of strength that I could muster. I barely cleared the road before the car flew by. Thank rabbits, I was safe! That car would have stopped for no one.

The falling snow was now piled deep. With each step I took, I sank into its depth up to my chest, exhausting me. All of a sudden, my attention was caught to the side of me by a boy carrying a rifle, walking in the snow. I was once shot at when I lingered too near a lamb, and the sight of the boy's rifle sent fear into me. I was afraid he would take aim at me, so I tried to avoid him. I thought I was safe, until I heard the crack of a rifle shot and a bullet whizzing by me. It had a special scary sound. I bounded away like crazy, utterly terrified. But there was no place to go. The few houses around would probably offer me more problems, like confronting another goose or someone else's gun. I began to think that maybe I had better find the place from which I had escaped. My master had taken me there and he must have trusted the boarding house to take care of me. They had done nothing bad to me. I had not been in pain and I was treated reasonably well. If my master was ever to find me again, I had better return to the original spot where he left me. But where to go? The shifting snow was no longer descending, but it was rapidly obliterating important smells and scents. I had to be honest with myself–I was totally lost. What could I do? Even though I had a thick coat of fur, the cold penetrated me.

But before I could worry any longer, a rabbit bounded before me. Now, this experience I liked; it was definitely interesting. I rushed at his tantalizing cottontail flashing before me and he went bobbing off into the brush. I was just behind. The deep snow really hindered me, while my esteemed quarry seemed to just skim over the snow's surface. I was losing ground and finally lost trace of him. Where was I now? I looked up to find my bearings when I discovered to my surprise that I stood at the entrance of the kennel. It was a lucky accident. I almost barked with joy. I trotted to the doorway and the male keeper found me immediately; he had been outside searching for me. He was most relieved. He repeated over and over that my owners were very upset when he had telephoned them about my disappearance, and now they would be glad to have me back. He said he would immediately contact them. More importantly, he complimented me on being a very smart dog. He led me inside and for the first and only time gave me some treats to eat.

Well, I waited it out. I knew my masters would arrive to fetch me. They did in good time and greeted me warmly, my mistress petting and stroking me, my master embarrassingly flopping on his knees to be on my level and kissing me. They apparently missed me. They also lauded me for my intelligence. However, I suspect they really doubted my mental ability and thought that I was lucky. Little do they know that when I was lost, I somehow managed to get involved in a rabbit chase that led me back. Whether I deserved it or not, I enjoyed the praise anyway.

When they brought me home, the angry man who pressured them to make me vacate my home was gone. I didn't get a chance to see his little girl. Too bad. Anyway, all ended well. I strongly doubt that my masters will allow me to ever leave home again. For my part, if my master continues to behave himself, I will gladly suffer myself to receive his silly kisses.

THE DIGNITARY

THE GUARDIAN MOUNTAIN WATCHES me as I make my daily rounds in the small town where I live. In fact, I feel that I am always in its focus and cannot escape its awesome scrutiny. Sometimes I think of Chester and the mountain, and I am wedged between both of them.

In our town we have no dignitaries to speak of, although there was a woman on Richard Nixon's enemy list who was investigated by the IRS. Nary a lord, duke or princess has claimed this town as theirs. We once had the brother of a famous Hollywood actress live here for awhile, but being a mere relation didn't give him the special status of a dignitary. Even a Hollywood actor, who dwelled among the angels of Los Angeles but periodically nestled within our boundaries, didn't qualify. Of course the real dignitaries are the Indian Pueblo leaders or those from the Hispanic community, but in the eyes of an official social register they do not qualify.

However, one man might fit the bill. Tall, heavyset, with coarse brown hair, his name was Chester E. Pratt. Although I knew it was not correct, I liked to think that E. stood for the word Equitable. Young and not much removed from a university, Chester managed to serve as the town's only philanthropist. Everyone could tell that he hailed from a wealthy family with good background and was endowed with an inheritance, the amount of which was always an engrossing topic of conversation among his friends. He was courteous and polite and made a special point to meet the local folks, even the hippies, who at that time were flourishing. He was conscious that he stood out from the majority, but he identified sympathetically with its interests and enjoyed its picturesque qualities. You could sense that Chester was a writer, or was aspiring to be one, since he actively observed people and their affairs, soaking up rich experiences and jotting them down. Often, though, I wondered if he wasn't more interested in himself and his own reactions to unfolding events than with the reactions of the people involved. He had a grand conception of himself, logging every thought and action in a personal mental notebook. He talked about himself as a giant actor on his own personal stage; all the people he encountered were his admiring audience. The splendid words he enjoyed using in conversation frequently awed his listeners, suggesting that if he could think them, he could write them down, verbal evidence of a rich vocabulary and a fine-tuned mind. Associated with his intellectual qualities was an impeccable taste in literature. I often visited him to get a new book to read. He would look down at me, stern and paternal, although I was decidedly older than he.

"Have you read Ford Maddox Ford's *Parade's End*? You were supposed to a week ago," he shot at me.

"I just finished it."

"And that's all?"

"As you said, except perhaps for Lady Macbeth, the novel portrays the most magnificent and evil woman in English literature."

"Right! She's almost evil for evil's sake. You are more than ready for my next recommendation: Wilkie Collins' *A Woman in White*, complete with great suspense and an incredibly evil male villain in an English vein. Here it is. Don't be late this time," and his command was coated with enticing mischievousness.

The philanthropist part of Chester made him particularly special to me. He bought large pieces of land and sold smaller pieces at cost with no interest to inhabitants who could otherwise not have afforded to own property. Then again, he made money by selling other parcels to outsiders as a profitable real estate investment. His scheme seemed to work. Furthermore, the village's youth center and football field were built on land deeded to it by Chester E. Pratt, a good deed equaled by his having a large, expensive house constructed for himself, built by villagers who were well paid.

My relationship with Chester came from mutual pursuits we shared. I pretended to be a writer, so we played at being poets and poeticizing, and we read the best books, saw elite movies whenever they reached our backwater town and ate superior food. We were concerned about the welfare of the town and county and wanted to contribute something meaningful. Even though I worked, I had spare time, and as Chester didn't need to work, we planned to offer some worthwhile service that hadn't existed before. Chester felt our educational advantages gave us special insight into the area's problems. It was his credo and it was all right with me. One way Chester figured we could benefit the townspeople was to be environmentalists, a priestly caste who could call attention to threatening communal problems and dangers.

Chester had connections with an environmental group at the state university one hundred miles south of town. He was a charter member and helped to finance the pioneer organization, an achievement that must not be forgotten, no matter what part he played at the end of our struggle. The issue Chester and our group faced was that the local ski industry was polluting the river, which started at the mountaintop and rushed down the slopes, passing through four old Hispanic villages situated below. A decrepit sewage plant built by the Forest Service could not handle the increasing waste load. When the Forest Service refused to build a new plant, the bustling ski industry abnegated its responsibility of constructing one. Instead, it devised a huge expansion project.

Alarmed, Chester immediately convened a meeting of those he respected and trusted to combat the coming threat. He explained that the industry wanted a right-of-way through Forest Service land to build a three-hundred-bed hotel at timberline above the present lodges. Simultaneously, a family-run business, the Ferguson Trust, owned land adjacent to the ski interest and needed the same right-of-way in order to reach and develop its considerable land holdings. The Trust had previously sold cabins located on land which had once provided the only safe passageway to their domain, and now the Trust couldn't or wouldn't buy back the cabins. Both parties pledged to work together and signed an agreement whereby, if the ski faction secured the road from the Forest Service, the Trust would give them some of its land as a bonus for its use of the right-of-way. Then the whole area would expand into a large, populated town.

Chester knew the pitfalls. He grumbled, "The problem is the Forest Service. It will allow both applicants what they want unless we apply pressure on the turkeys and take the issue to the public. What we need is time and the Forest Service isn't willing to allow us any—only two days to act. It is already using its employees to clear the road in anticipation of granting the right-of-way." Chester steamed and pointed out that it is against the law for any Federal Government agency to use public moneys to aid a private enterprise. He turned to me and said, "I recommend you see the regional Forest Service supervisor and press him to delay making any immediate decision."

The next afternoon I sat before Emory Anderson, who in company uniform stared at me from across his desk. I gazed back.

He was a veteran, hard-boiled administrator, fully immersed in the bureaucracy. I wanted Anderson to divulge the Forest Service's position on the road, and I knew that in order to get answers, I would have to pester him with questions, even if it irritated him, since he would not voluntarily give information. "Mr. Anderson," I began, "this stretch of public road you want to donate to the ski developers, shouldn't there be a public review to see if it's in the best interests of the public? What's the name of that review?" I asked, even though I knew the answer.

"An environmental impact statement," he said matter-of-factly.

"Oh, right, I think we should have that."

"But it's not needed," he said authoritatively. "This is a routine matter."

"What do you mean it's a routine matter?" I said. "I don't understand."

A fly of annoyance landed on his face. "I mean an environmental impact statement is simply not required. This is just a right-of-way request. We don't need an EIS."

"What?" I said, feigning shock. "You mean you can give public land away without doing anything, without public input or investigation?"

"Yes, we can, yes indeed," he said, "if it involves small parcels of land for public recreational purposes. No big deal."

Amazed, I said, "And you don't have to do anything? You can just give it away?"

"Well," he said, "we do have to check out the flora and fauna."

"The flora and fauna," I said. "Why do you have to check out the flora and fauna?"

Vexed by my question, he replied, "We are required by law to see if there's anything of biological or geological value that would be disturbed by granting a right-of-way."

"What would have to be disturbed?"

He glared at me. "An endangered species. But," he said firmly, "no endangered species are present there."

"So you are telling me," I said, glaring back, "that if there are no endangered species, then the ski developers get the road, even though there is an enormous problem with this decision?"

"What problem? There is no problem."

"Yes, there is," I said. "What has walking the road and checking out the flora and fauna got to do with handing that road over to these businesses, which will then mushroom in size and wealth, bringing with them thousands of people, who will further pollute the river and atmosphere? Why should you be pushing this? Why should public land be used at all?"

Anderson stiffened and leaned forward. "All we are required to do is examine the land. Our decision is based solely on biological and geological data. Period. If there are no endangered species, the applicants get the road. Period. We do not need to waste the taxpayer's money on an EIS when all we have to do is walk the road. The ski industry is a Forest Service permittee. Nothing can stop our granting a small section of road to them. This is normal procedure. Do you understand?"

"Just sticks, pebbles, gullies, worms and a couple of nesting birds- these are your facts? Your scientific data? You want to make sure they are all there? Is that all you care about?"

"Exactly," Anderson smiled.

"But it is not just a plain road. What's important is what the road will be used for and whose interests it will serve. The road is the only means by which more commercial development can take place, and you know it. These are the more important facts, not the sticks and stones and bunches of bushes. You are furthering the growth of the ski valley at the expense of the mountain and the Hispanic villages below. You are endangering the Pueblo's sacred ceremonial land. The Forest Service is supposed to represent the public welfare. There is no justification for you to give the road to private exploiters. Why isn't that your major concern?"

Anderson flicked his hand downward with a deprecatory gesture. He had had enough. Disdainfully he asked, "Who is in this protest with you?"

"Chester Pratt," I said, recognizing the altercation, or rather the charade, had ended.

Reflecting only an instant he attempted to smile. "You have a good man, by and large, and I think, a community leader. He is not a rabble-rouser." Then he sobered, "There are just two days left for you to get back to me. That's it. No extension."

Immediately I went to see Chester and with a heavy heart reported that I had not obtained a delay from the supervisor. Chester chuckled. "Anderson is not the most intelligent government official we've met," he said. "All he would have had to do is grant you a little more time, a token extension, and that would have shut you up. But it would not have really helped. We still would not have had enough time to generate any effective opposition. Anderson would still have had his way."

"What about the district supervisor?" I inquired. "I hear he's more sensitive to our interests."

"Good idea," Chester replied. "Call him. You do know, I hope," he said, "that if you fail, we've had it." I knew it and then departed, determined to succeed.

That afternoon I telephoned the district supervisor at his headquarters and explained that we, the opposition, had not even had time to put an article in the local newspaper to inform the public of what was happening. He instantly saw my point and granted a two week extension. I was elated. When I passed Supervisor Anderson in the post office later that day, he hissed, "So you went behind my back, did you?" I laughed and nodded, feeling I had truly earned my place as a teammate of Chester Pratt. Jubilant, I called Chester to tell him the good news. He congratulated me and said I was his number-one lieutenant.

I immediately wrote an article for the town newspaper, but as it was published only once a week, we came up with the idea of holding a public forum, an open community hearing to discuss the issues. Chester wanted to be chairman, saying that if he assumed that position he could control the flow of events. "Not only will I choose who is to speak, and in which order, but I can freely comment on anything I want," he said, "which will help our cause. I'll call the Forest Service and set up a time and place." Convinced that Chester was a master showman with a master's mind, I asked a friend of mine, Ernie Hogarth, a black, bushy-haired photographer, to help schedule announcements with the radio station and to prepare advertisements. I posted handmade bulletins at strategic places in town.

We had agreed to convene before the evening's meeting, and Chester invited Ernie and me and our wives to dinner. When we arrived at the restaurant, over-dressed to please Chester, he greeted us and introduced us to the sophisticated young woman we had heard he was dating. He had also invited an attorney he had hired, Mac Rogers, an expert in environmental law, one of only a few in the region. I was fascinated by Chester's woman friend, who complemented him perfectly. She was quiet and yet supportive, nodding tiny assents to his assertions and patting him approvingly on the arm. She was stylishly dressed, especially compared to the rather informal natives, and although she was not what I would call beautiful, the more I glanced at her thin, tall frame and her poise and easy manners (and glance I did), the more attractive I thought she was. To me, it once more proved that Chester had good taste.

"May this meeting come to disorder, good spirits and lusty appetites," Chester toasted. "May we win the battle in the saddle." Chester was both cheerful and businesslike, and often during the conversation he checked with his lawyer on technical points. He told us that the auditorium was bound to be filled, just as we desired, and that the town was curious and could be guided to ask the Forest Service for yet another delay. And then he leaned over and put his finger to his mouth. "Shhhh, me thinks we should tone our voices down a notch so that our battle plans cannot be overheard by potential non-believers around us." We became aware of the dozen other diners sitting near us.

He was obviously enjoying himself. "We should add a sense of drama to these rather drab proceedings. Tonight's foray is only a beginning. The audience isn't about to choose sides tonight. I know, I've been to similar meetings before. We have to set up a campaign. I need reliable troops to carry out important assignments. You," he said, taking my arm, "you be the bad guy, the hard-core opposition. Ask for an environmental impact statement. This is really standard procedure but, at this point, you will represent the worse possible course of action to the ski group and one that would freeze all their expansion plans for at least a year. Don't look so surprised. You are a natural when it comes to being vehemently against something." I wondered at first how to take that, but on reflection I thought he was complimenting me on being a good fighter.

"As for you, Ernie, you should be a moderating force. You should politely ask the ski people to fix their broken-down plant and stop its pollution. Put them on the defensive. And you can reinforce him," he said, pointing to my wife. "If you launch a concerted attack on the group's ski units and the Trust's real estate business, they will have to make some concessions. You have to create a big stir." We sat engrossed as he formulated his grand strategy.

Holding out his big hands, he leaned back and said, "Sometimes everything is going along so smoothly for me I feel that I have found my true calling–being an environmental activist. All the manipulating I do is quite natural. It's similar to the facile talents of the character Kane in Orson Wells' film, *Citizen Kane*, and along with Kane, I like to be liked."

During Chester's seemingly charming preamble, I uneasily began to view him in a different light. I disliked his use of military terms and his demanding attitude. However, much more disconcerting was that the merchant who ran a store I patronized ignored me and turned away when I said hello. Equally, a motel owner whom I waved to just stared at me and didn't respond. As we were leaving, I realized that these people whom I considered to be friends, or certainly friendly, were going to the meeting and all of them knew I was an environmentalist. To them my involvement would be negative, against businessmen making money, even though I was a businessman. I realized then that I was, in fact, a free man. I didn't have to depend on the town and its businessmen for any commercial success, since I was able to sell most of my merchandise out of state. Therefore I would survive.

Chester paid the bill. Ernie and I did not object because we thought it fulfilled his proper princely role. We walked across the square to the auditorium, and as night fell I looked up at the huge mountain guarding the town, wrapped in its mantle of dark blue. I felt it was my personal friend. Somewhat comforted, I walked on but still imagined people turning their eyes inward in order not to see me. My paranoia was relieved when friends greeted me and supporters began to assemble. As Chester predicted, the auditorium was packed. Someone went over to the windows and lifted them one by one, helping to alleviate the hot summer air that mingled with cigarette smoke.

Chester stood confidently before us. He had buttoned his handsome, expensive sport coat, and before he began his introductory remarks, his figure took on an expansive air. In front of him he spotted the town's mayor, a group of Pueblo Indians, members of the ski group and the Ferguson Trust, Forest Supervisor Anderson and his disciples, a large group of businessmen and a scattering of sympathizers.

"I am Chester Pratt," he announced. "Those who know me maybe shouldn't, and those who don't are stuck with me this evening." The crowd laughed. "I represent myself and regard myself as a concerned citizen. I know you people here tonight would normally be playing chess or be engaged in fencing or performing a Japanese tea ceremony–you would not be watching television, not at any cost. But seriously, I feel you are as interested as I am in these matters."

The audience was amused. Chester had a light touch and had caught the crowd's attention. "I am here as a mediator," he continued, "to help work out solutions to these important problems, but I can only succeed with your active partnership, only if you become involved in this affair. I have a mandate from the various parties in this room to reach a consensus or a compromise. That would be a good thing to bring about."

A light shower of clapping and a few shouts of encouragement ensued.

When we heard that, Ernie and I pricked up our ears. "What's going on?" Ernie whispered to me, "What mandate?"

Chester had begun to smoothly conduct the audience like an orchestra. He asked me to speak first, and I wished he hadn't. I rumbled and burbled my complaint. I said that before the right-of-way was granted, an environmental impact statement was needed. Not unexpectedly, some muffled boos were heard. Before I had finished, Chester interrupted and said, "Let the others have a chance," and called on the next speaker. I was taken aback and somewhat humiliated but thought that, in order to prove his impartiality, he had decided to treat me in an indifferent manner.

He called on the mayor, who wanted the Hispanic villages downstream to be protected, and Chester, asserting his friendship with the Hispanics, agreed with his statement. The ski industry official was next, who said the requested three hundred hotel units and the right-of-way for the road would produce an economic boom for the region. Like he was God, Chester agreed to the new right-of-way and to the units but said the right-of-way should go only as far as the ski valley, not to the Trust land. The ski officials were silently pleased. Although the Ferguson people were surprised and confused, they also went along with the plan. Chester was content. The Indian Pueblo spokesman stated that allowing the road right-of-way and development would cause crowds of people to trespass on sacred Indian grounds and despoil them with trash. Chester responded that since there would be no development on the Ferguson land next to the Pueblo, the Forest Service would be able to protect the Indian boundaries from trespass. The Ferguson Trust did not object. Puzzled by the Trust's acquiescence, Ernie and I raised our eyebrows and looked at each other. I figured the Trust was going to somehow be rewarded, probably under the table.

Chester was moving swiftly, scoring points and winning over islands of recalcitrant doubters, cajoling, cheering, acting grave and extraordinarily responsible and sympathetic, even assuming a posture of simple humility. When Ernie's turn arrived, he began to speak about the ski investors' pollution, according to Chester's instructions, but Chester turned away and looked out the window, ignoring Ernie. He cut Ernie short. His eyes widened with acute impatience and he called for no further bickering. Embarrassed, Ernie sat down. I began to feel ill inside. My wife then popped up and inquired, "Should the ski people be rewarded for polluting the river by letting them have access to the public's road? Or, should they instead be fined by the state and federal governments?" Chester's large, heavy frame turned toward this disturbance, his dark, explosive eyes intensely working on her. He declared her to be out of order. At that, the audience burst into applause. The last remnants of our wastrel army of opposition wilted. Masterfully, Chester had cast a spell of false conciliation over the audience. He was clearly in control. Ernie's wife whispered to mine that Chester appeared about to pull the rabbit out of the hat, but which rabbit and which hat, and which Chester?

In one deft stroke Chester fit together all the pieces in his plan. An agreement was wrought with all responsible parties bound to its terms. The ski group could construct all its ski units but the Trust would keep its land free of development, thus satisfying the Indians. If the mayor would forbear criticism of the pollution for a few years, the ski enterprise would be in a position to build a new super sewage treatment plant to handle their units, old and new, provided it was technologically possible. It was all there, the harmony of a logically perfect agreement. Beyond expectation, Chester had set a precedent and garnered what no other environmentalist had accomplished. He had conceived and implemented a compact that would be signed by five parties, woven, incredibly, of five strands of different colors: the Town Fathers, the ski developers, the Trust, the Indians and supposedly us, the not-so-honorable opposition, caught in the skein. The magic number was five.

I sat bathed in numbness. I thought: It simply amounts to the mountain. Only the mountain. They will continue to soil it daily, staining it with a dark evil, or to wear it down. I can almost hear the roar of flushed waste gushing in its river. Everything's a waste.

Ernie and I and our wives quickly slid off the bench and headed for the door. I saw Chester's woman friend and Anderson congratulate Chester. We chose an exit free of Chester and his friends. The evening had turned bitterly cold. Walking swiftly, Chester came up to us.

"I hope you appreciate how delicate tonight's proceedings were," he said arrogantly. "The audience would have let the Forest Service grant the road to both the ski group and the Trust, so the meeting had to be intelligently led. I think I managed the whole affair reasonably well."

"But you lied to us!" I shouted. "You didn't represent us at all. You're an impostor. You gave away the mountain. The ski industry gets three hundred hotel units. Three hundred! That was the worst concession. It means the whole mountain. Why did you have to do that? Why? We were just your pawns, manipulated by you to satisfy your illusions of grandeur."

"You do not understand," he said grimly. "Yes, there were certain trade-offs. Some give and take. But the Trust cannot build on top of the mountain. There won't be any unlimited septic tanks, which would be far worse than the ski interest's controlled sewage treatment plant. And you people, what do you ever accomplish? Nothing. You have to compromise in this business to save your skin, to salvage a few crumbs. You're just a bunch of emotional asshole losers. If I hadn't intervened, you would have been duped by the Forest Service and won not a damn thing."

My wife leveled softly, "But you're no hero. With all your pretensions, you sold out."

He regarded us with disdain. "Sell your mountain, did I? Well, I think you blissful souls should understand this. Before the battle is over, you're going to lose several mountains and a couple of seas, too, and maybe some clouds before we're through. You have to lose! We always have to lose! Eventually, losing is the name of this game. But you have to know how to minimize the loss. This is the last time I'm going to help you fools." He turned away from us, trying to control his rage.

And there went my friend, Chester E. Pratt, fading away in the cold night, fading away from us forever, the only dignitary we ever had.

TURF

THE GODS CONVENED. THEY SAT down for supper and looked below on mortal earth to find entertainment. They spotted an eleven year-old boy, lithe and freckled, with yellow-brown hair, not especially arresting physically.

On his turf, Cody Williams was concluding his daily one mile walk from Carthay Circle Elementary School in West Los Angeles through a middle class block of pseudo-Spanish, tile-roofed, stucco houses. This street, a couple of blocks from his house, was where he and his friends played football almost every day. Cody usually worked his way home in peace, except on an occasional day when he had to circumvent Al, who now stood before him.

Al! Menacing Al. Wherever Al was, was his territory. He was a squat tub who had flunked the sixth grade twice and who exuded blind bravado, which let him thoroughly whip every challenger. Al, and one, two, three, four minor Als, a bunch of carbon copy Als, opposed Cody.

Al declared, "This street is my street and you're pissing on it-pissing on my parade. Move over to the other side so we can get by, and scram out of here. Out of our way, asshole."

"This is not your block and you don't belong here," Cody defied him. "It is where I live and my friends play here. You have nothing to do with this place, so get out."

"Nobody gives Al orders. Al doesn't obey any fucking orders. Al tells you what to do. That's the law here," he growled and cocked his fist.

"You can't make me move."

"Okay, you want trouble, that's what you want? Well, you're gonna eat enough trouble until it covers your whole face." His eyebrows drooped and his neck lowered like a bull's. "I'll bust your balls!" With heavy chopping strides he thrust forward within inches of Cody.

Even the Gods, watching intently, considered Al a formidable force, especially his mouthing of such terrible oaths, in which They excelled. They realized Cody's next decision was critical.

Sizing up Al, Cody capitulated and headed for the opposite sidewalk.

"Good boy," Al cheered. "Be a good boy and do what Al tells you, or you're gonna get killed. All Al has to do is let this little bomb explode (circling his fists threateningly) and you'll never get up again."

Cody stuck to silence. The mob jeered and passed triumphantly on what was once his street and was now theirs. One of them gave him the finger skyward, straight up, firm as a ramrod. Leaving the street in anguish, Cody slowly trudged home.

The Gods, viewing Cody's retreat, came to an agreement. "Now!" They exclaimed. "Now!"

Abruptly Cody stopped, hulked on his heels and slowly pivoted.

"Hey, you guys, wait a minute," he screamed, stretching his vocal chords. "I am not afraid of you anymore! Forget it. Come back."

Al and company halted, sneered, took measure of the bawling fool and waited to see what the idiot would do next.

"I meant what I said. I am going across the street. I am taking over this block."

At the end of his clarion battle call, Cody performed a deed of naked aggression. He boldly entered the disputed territory and claimed it.

The group shook its collective head in disbelief at Cody's brazen war declaration. The multi-headed monster swung around and clumped toward Cody, whose courage plummeted. He thought, why? Why did I do what I just did? Just dumb.

His opponents came with confidence curled on their lips. But Cody knew his strength. He was the fastest runner in his school, along with Jackie Larson. He could run so fast he was a blur. But he could also fight, if he had to prove the point. Yes, he could.

The adversaries met. Al disengaged from the scowling pack, threw his sweater to his brothers and sauntered into the arena with calculated indifference.

Cody danced with invisible springs tied to his feet, up and down. His light body, half the weight of Al's, pranced. To Al, Cody, with his zany, unmanly antics, behaved like a weakling. Irritated, Al's chorus heckled the ridiculous windup toy that made them dizzy.

"Listen to me," Al tore a glance to his supporters. "This jumping jack wants to fight. Should we give him what he wants? Should we be so nice?"

"Let him have it!" "Beat the shit out of him!" "Flatten him."

Al turned snide. "Here I am, like you asked for. Just little me. If you will stay still for a second, we can do something about having a real fight. Stop your bobbing up and down before you get tired!" Hands fluttering by his side, Al stood like an unalterable lump.

Cody circled him, pedaling, backpedaling, weaving in and out and continually jabbing short staccato punches, mesmerizing Al. Suddenly, violently, his coiled left hand jab lengthened in a surprise attack, followed by a right uppercut and a brick-hard strike. He continued to hammer blows on Al's astonished and now bruised face. Al staggered and fell backward, sitting crudely on his ass. Red welts disfigured his mouth, cheeks and forehead.

Cody continued to dance around his stricken foe as if he was an automaton propelled by some bizarre force he could not stop.

Al, still floored, rubbed his wounds while his eyes blazed at Cody with baleful ire. "All right, you saw it. He took advantage of me when my hands were down and I wasn't ready to fight. I thought he was fooling around, dancing. Now I need help. Do you hear me? Why don't you pansies come here and cream him. Tear him to pieces. Just break his damn neck."

Their leader had failed them, and now it was the band's turn to do battle. Hesitantly agreeing, they closed in on Cody.

The most serious disaster was heading toward him, and Cody watched the enemy slowly approach. Given their determined numbers, Cody knew he would be clobbered. Al scrambled to his feet and joined his comrades, this time as an ordinary trooper without any special status. The bunch pressed onward, ejecting hoots, shrieks and other spirited sounds. Cody stepped back; doom was so close he could smell it.

Nodding Their heads in unison, the Gods concurred that the time had arrived for Them to intervene.

Deus ex machina then materialized. Cody's mother appeared down the street in her black 1938 Buick sedan on the way home. Much to her horror, she spotted the mortal contest. She decided to halt the predictable ebb of events which decreed that her only son would be subjected to a brutal and unfair thrashing. She stepped out of the car, a tall, gaunt, imperious woman in her fifties, who dominated the scene like a heron towering over a marsh of abject underwater creatures. With this singular appearance she ended the conflict. Routed in disarray, the boy army disappeared with hardly a snort, streaming away in the opposite direction and restoring the street to Cody.

In the car Cody sternly questioned his mother. "Mom, why did you have to ruin things the way you always ruin things by interfering with what I do? You embarrassed me in front of those guys. You should have left me alone. It was my fight. I'd have done all right."

"Cody, if you prefer, I will turn around and drive right back and let you out to handle those boys as you wish," she replied. "Is that what you want? How stupid. I just happened to drive up in the nick of time. That was a gift from heaven. You're really lucky."

He was noticeably silent. "Mom, I beat Al in a fight," he finally declared.

"At least I did that all on my own," and he looked proud.

"Good for you," she smiled, patting him on the shoulder. "I am so glad that you won, and I am glad you did it on your own-your very own."

The Gods clapped Their hands softly.

THE CAGE

ALTHOUGH NOT A BIRD WATCHER, I gravitate toward birds. Under a gray, cold-ruffled Alaskan sky in the late afternoon, I was seeking the rehabilitation center for birds which I had seen advertised. Before me was a domed fence enclosure surrounding a fifty-yard-long metal tunnel, seemingly empty and dormant. But suddenly I noticed the disturbing white-headed body. The enormous bird, a bald eagle, moved not a muscle but stared intensely ahead, probably not just at me, although I was only a few yards away. Yet I felt the space between us electrified by the force of its pinwheel eyes bearing down on me. By its side was a second eagle, less alert, less robust, fluttering in disarray. It shifted its body uneasily and jerked and swiveled its head, while its eyes darted in many directions, unable to focus on their target. Both birds were dense, crucial, unbearable. Their snow-white heads contrasted with their bulks held together by large envelopes of dark brown feathers, tinged with splotches of cream white. Behind them, on the ground, a wounded, smaller and younger eagle scuttled awkwardly, flapping its wings pathetically.

From a building in back of their cage emerged a slender, diminutive man wearing a dark, drab, loosely fitting coat, and as he neared, I thought he might be an Eskimo or a Northwest Indian. His tight dark hair capped a sweet, benign face. He took small, soft steps. Nodding to me, he opened the door, stepped in and then paused before the birds. With no warning this demure man exploded. His arms thrashed and swung and flailed about, and he screamed and yelled in piercing tones, threatening the birds. Aroused and alarmed, they turned and flapped their large, out-stretched wings and stridently beat the air. They cast off in a straight, low trajectory, flying through the tunnel to the other side, where they slammed ferociously into the fencing, causing their wings to collapse, while their talons stabbed at the unyielding iron mesh and wildly clutched it. Within seconds they turned around and catapulted themselves onto a high wooden bench, where they resumed their immutable pose. During the flurry, the man tracked the birds through the tunnel to the other side and there repeated the same procedure, exciting them and forcing them to take flight. Again they crash-landed into the wire fence, crazed and bewildered, but soon they regained their former composure.

Catching his breath the man glanced at me.

"Why do you do that?" I asked.

He faced me but kept his attention on the birds. "They have to have exercise in this cage. They are sick and hurt, and a vital part of healing them is to prod them to fly, to make them get used to using their wings again, so they can be set free to compete in the wilds."

"Hurt and sick? How?"

"Injured by bullets, baited traps and electronic fences, and poisoned by pesticides. It's a hard fate."

"Is this your job, watching birds? If so, fine job."

He shook his head. "Not exactly. For now I'm their keeper and I look after them. This place is like a sanitarium for birds."

"Do you live here?" I continued.

"No, I come here every day to help the birds. I actually live in town, next to the Russian Orthodox Church."

"The Russian church?" For some reason I felt uneasy at his mention of the church.

"The same," he affirmed. "For the native people and practically everyone else, that is basically the only church in town. I consider this spot a church for birds. It's part of my training to become an orthodox priest. I study and also receive instruction from my superior, and in a year I hope to take my orders."

"Can you really preside over a church for birds?"

He answered, "Like us, I think these creatures are also creatures of God. They, too, are His emblems. Little bits of God. We all have the same pulse of life. Like us, I feel these birds need the aid of Jesus. Life has been cruel to them. I am not yet a priest, but I can still administer to a flock, literally this flock; and if I can cure the sick and wounded, they can fly away into the bosom of God."

During his explanation, I had an impulse to look over at the birds. When he said "God," I glanced at their leathery skin-crinkled claws; at the word "Jesus," I noticed the yellow murder-powered beak; and when "priest" was uttered, I saw their bouldered contours.

"The smaller bird on the ground is in bad shape." I questioned, "Will he recover?"

"Highly improbable," he replied. "He has DDT poisoning, which is usually lethal. At least he's alive. The bird there that is in the best condition I believe will survive and be able to fly, if he gets enough exercise. The other one is quite damaged. His timing and reactions are off. A bullet shattered a nerve center. He has a chance."

Observing the wild beasts, I felt they were not confined by the cage of our own beliefs. They more likely cared about wind and rain and cloud and star, their first tenets of some inner wisdom that the church of man could not translate.

"You have to understand our feathered friends," he stated. "They have souls, too. But I must go now and stir them up and off another time. Make a lot of commotion. This is what they need."

"Keep up the good work."

The man turned back to the cage. "All in good time."

As I watched them for a moment, I thought: clearly the birds understandeth not.

EACH DAY I HUNT

O IS FOR OBSESSION, A MENTAL STATE that perfectly describes me. I crave art, collect it, fondle it and almost devour it. Naturally, my home is a repository for my collection, or perhaps from another point of view, a rich tomb in which to be buried. Each day I hunt for an irresistible gem of tribal art that waits to surprise and seize me. To seek, find and acquire artistic objects is a role I believe I was created for. All my talents are honed to make such discoveries, and like a spider I spin my web to grasp what treasure I can capture. By their intrinsic aesthetic nature all masterpieces that exist outside our awareness are waiting to receive from us their due recognition and appreciation. We are the losers if we do not accord them their rights. They do not need us because they are inviolate in greatness.

On a day of no particular merit, a minor friend of mine, Jonas Spaulding, visited me. I thought: as an accountant he mismanaged my affairs, but still the old duffer was shrewd enough to see that I had a successful business and copied me by investing in Southwest American Indian pots.

He focused on prehistoric pottery and bought within his means, a feat I often couldn't achieve. He must have a reason to be here.

"You realize you have influenced me to collect a lot of stuff," he complained and gawked as he scanned my crowded walls. "Stuff to others, I guess, but to me special creations. I can't afford to buy on an accountant's income, but I am hooked on these things and there is no way out."

"Jonas," I said, "you're now a good dealer, so good that you have me buying from you." This I considered to be a compliment. "Have you anything for me?"

"No. I'm here because I was passing through Dove Creek in Colorado and stopped to have coffee with Brian Bates. You know him; he handles early pottery. He told me that he happened to have a group of old Northern New Mexico santos, thirty of them, both the flat, painted boards and the figures, and they were for sale for $30,000. I asked him if he had contacted you, since you collect them. He said to me, looking quite serious, 'I will not sell anything to Sandy Harrow,' and he meant it. I thought you should know."

"Brian Bates has good taste," I jumped in, stung by the remark. "He must be mad at me because I never bought anything from him when he was a dealer in Los Angeles. He probably thinks I'm not worth bothering with. But, hell, I didn't have any money then. I guess I am completely off his list."

"You sure are. No question about it. And he has outstanding pieces, too," Jonas readily agreed.

"Yes, damn it. Has he married or does he still live alone?" I asked.

"No, he hasn't married. It seems like he has always taken care of his old mother and father as long as I have know him. He is forty and single, and I've heard he is a perfect mamma's boy."

"Thanks for the tip. Maybe I can win him over, but I don't see how."

So, so, wiggle my toe, I agitated; thirty New Mexico santos lurk somewhere out of my grasp, probably all exquisite. I looked up at my wall where I had a few jewels. To me they were the American equivalent of medieval religious art. Where should I begin? Bates might be adamant, but he was also greedy. The $30,000 came to mind; start there. Suppose I went to the bank and withdrew that exact amount and bought a cashier's check. Then

I could strike. I could hire Abel Laker to fly me to Dove Creek. But what if Bates was not there? Better have someone else call him for an appointment to be sure he would be around. Somebody from New York City sounds impressive. And pin him down to a definite time in the morning. No slip-ups. But what if the santos were of poor quality or were fakes? No, I decided, with Brian's taste the collection had to be excellent.

Abel Laker consented to fly me, and a female friend telephoned Brian Bates for an appointment at ten the next morning. At five I left my house and a half an hour later Abel and I taxied down the runway. The single engine plane had a compartment in back large enough to store the works of beauty that I hoped to extract from my unsuspecting victim. I tried to convince myself that my scheme was more plus than minus and not a streak of madness.

The plane flew over the rock pinnacles struggling up from the floor of Monument Valley, and Abel gave me fits by dropping low and skimming past them. When we landed I repeated my traditional blessing: "Thank you for saving the rest of my middle-aged life."

"Not at all. It's quite routine," he replied.

To our surprise the small airport at Dove Creek was a barren oasis with no planes on the ground, and upon landing we realized there was no one attending it. We were some distance from town. Abel commented that a mangy airport like this usually belongs to a mangy town.

After walking to the main road, we tried to hitch a ride into town. No one stopped for awhile but finally we were picked up by a garage mechanic. The delay didn't hurt us because Bates' shop wouldn't open for another hour. When we arrived, we inquired about the shop and were told it was on the corner of the plaza. Directly across from it stood a dingy cafe where we ordered black coffee. We had forty-five minutes to compose ourselves and look out the window at the people passing by.

"Can you recognize him?" Abel asked.

Yes," I nodded. "He is short, dumpy, flabby, with gray hair–about forty."

I took the cashier's check out of my wallet and put it in my shirt pocket. I was ready. Abel had a second cup and he, too, seemed primed. From around a corner, heading for the shop, waddled a nondescript, soft-contoured man who stood out to us like a neon sign.

"Let's go." I lurched from the table and put down a few coins for the waitress. "We must follow right behind him and catch him as he enters the shop."

Swiftly and cautiously we moved around the plaza, hugging rails and walls, slipping into doorways and entrances, keeping behind him, unseen. He stopped, took his keys from his pocket and fumbled at the keyhole, while we crept up from behind. As he opened the door and strode in, we were breathing down his neck. We all spilled into the shop at the same time.

"Brian," I announced, "here is a cashier's check for $30,000 for that group of thirty New Mexico santos you have for sale."

He dropped his keys. In a rush of action, he turned, blanched, flopped his mouth open and stroked his tousled hair in disbelief. His eyes bulged with astonishment. The door stood wide open. "What are you doing here?" he gasped. "You should not have come here without warning!"

"Here is my check, Brian, here take it; it's $30,000 cash. I have met your price; now I get the santos. It's a simple business arrangement." He grasped the check in trembling fingers.

"Good grief! What's happening? I can't believe it!" he said and sagged into a chair. "Well," he stammered, "you think I have santos-yes, you are right, although I can't figure out how you found out. You must want them badly." He got up and closed the door and then sat down again, stunned. "I had assembled the pieces one by one, starting when I was in Los Angeles. The idea was to form a significant collection for sale. Then I fell in love with them. The collection is still at my parents' home. I never brought them to the shop. Just recently I asked my mother whether I should keep them. She said I could sell. Otherwise I wouldn't."

I looked around the room and checked out his excellent Indian goods-historic Pueblo Indian pots, California baskets, Navajo blankets, but no New Mexico santos. He caught my taking stock.

"As I told you, the santos are not here; they are at my parents' house.

I have to go get them. But," and he paused, "I don't have thirty of them. In fact, I own only twenty-three, all great, as you undoubtedly know."

"But I paid you for the thirty santos I thought you had. It looks like you owe me some money back."

Brian revived. "No. I don't hold with that," he asserted, his short arms fluttering up and down. "You concluded you could buy my collection as if it was not necessary to consult me. There are twenty-three pieces and no more. You got the number wrong. I can give you back your check."

"I could be wrong," I acknowledged, "but I was told by a good source you had thirty items. My friend was clear about that."

"Whatever," he shrugged, "my santos are priced at $30,000. Twenty-three of them. You must decide for yourself."

Although I was confused, I reluctantly accepted his new terms. I intended to keep most of the santos for my collection and did not mind paying more. It was still a reasonable price, although there was no real profit left in the ones I might choose to sell. However, just to be able to obtain this collection and actually live with them in my house eased my concern. Plus, he had me. He knew that if I had come all the way to buy his material unseen, he had me hooked.

"Fine with me." Simulating a smile, I shook my head. "Bring on the santos. We have a deal-done. Let me go with you to pick them up."

"Oh, no," he stammered, "my parents are old and I try to protect them from the tensions of business. Poor dear souls, they are so good and pure they wouldn't understand what motivates us traders and dealers," and he gave a slight laugh. "I'll meet you here after lunch at two o'clock with the santos."

During lunch I unraveled my concern to Abel. "I heard my accountant right, I think, but perhaps he, and probably I, were a little vague at the time. Anyway, it's all over now and I struck gold. Even if I paid too much, I got what I wanted. Wow! We certainly shocked him when we barged into his shop. He was frazzled. My plan went perfectly."

"Maybe so, but he isn't as dumb as he looks," Abel counseled.

At the designated hour, I arrived. Bates had the santos arrayed, precisely twenty-three authentic examples of New Mexico saints, creating an exhilarating atmosphere that entirely transfigured the place.

Peopled perfectly, radiating verve and color, the saints reigned. The figures appealed so directly in their innocence and purity of expression that I lost my breath: a tall, linear San Miguel with fierce strength stepping on a dragon, San José plaintively nestling the tiny Christ child and San Rafael, the fisherman who casts for people's souls. These were accompanied by paintings on wood of a radiant Virgin Mary, Santa Barbara next to the tower in which she was once imprisoned and a stunning black-robed Santa Rita holding a bleached-white skull. Incredibly, they were far better than I had imagined.

"They are superb," I enthused. "It's an important group. I'm thrilled that I bought them." I loved that the whole escapade had proceeded so smoothly.

"You should be, considering the impossible circumstances you are putting me through," he snapped. "I should have prevented this from the start."

I decided that, since it was too late to fly back home that day, we would stay over in a hotel. Bates promised he would load the santos in his station wagon the next day and carry them to the plane.

"Our game of wheeling and dealing is over." He relaxed a bit. "Now we don't have to work so hard. So you've bought from me at last. We've done a deal. Aside from business, what I like to do best is study the Basketmakers. Their ruins are all around here. Ever been to Snake Gulch?"

He caught me by surprise. I did not want to become a friend. It was pointless. I was more comfortable with our adversarial relationship.

"The gulch with snakes?"

"That's not at all the point." He became serious, ignoring my foolish remark. "It has priceless Basketmaker pictographs. I will take you to them."

It was always in the back of my mind that Brian wouldn't have done business with me if I hadn't forced my way into his store. He probably resented my intrusion. But his offer to show me fine prehistoric rock paintings was an act of friendship, which, considering his ardor for his subject, I shouldn't squelch. However, in spite of my best effort to resist temptation, all this sober man provoked from me was an unadulterated desire to do mischief. Now why should his sudden introduction of Basketmaker art be taken seriously? And, besides, they couldn't be bought, sold or collected.

"You are talking about pictures by people who were working at the end of the Roman Empire," I stated. "Compared to the artists of that time in Europe, your Indians were primitive and had no particular artistic ability." Immediately, almost before my words became history, I wished I could have withdrawn them. Why was I so flippant with my far-fetched mention of the Roman Empire? He wouldn't understand my absurd irony, and why didn't I show him at least a measure of scholarly respect?

"You are off the mark." He was completely absorbed in thought. "The Romans are the Romans and the Basketmakers are the Basketmakers, two completely different cultures, and you cannot compare them. They both excelled, and the Basketmakers should be better known. To me they are famous. You'll find out for yourself."

Of course he was right, I understood that. What was worse, he knew Roman art and I was out of my depth with Basketmaker art. I should have instantly said yes to his offer and avoided all this fuss. I hated to become so involved with him.

"Let me make it simple," I made amends. "I should like to join you tomorrow and share the pictographs. Okay? It will be my pleasure. But what about the snakes in Snake Gulch? Are there any?"

"Plenty, all around, and if the weather is warm, all the worse. Rattlesnakes like to come out when it's warm. Be careful. There are diamondbacks."

Arrangements were made to meet him at his shop the next morning and from there we would proceed to the site in his jeep.

That night I dreamed heavily, not about the Basketmakers, but about snakes, a steady rivulet of them. The place was virtually a snakedom of venom and writhing. When the hissing commotion was at its worst, the santos miraculously appeared and engaged in battle with the reptiles. I woke up before the victor emerged. I left early; Abel stayed behind.

Taking sandwiches and cold drinks, we headed toward the cliffs. Brian meticulously drove his jeep over the dirt road, through high desert and past varied rock formations. Half addressing me and half speaking to the scattered trees, he mumbled, "It's a riddle to me-you and those santos. How did you know?"

"The unknowable, Brian," I teased, "there will always be the unknown, and I hope no snakes."

We entered a small canyon sprinkled with spiky green bushes. Brian stopped the car, got out, carefully looked around, and then walked to a cliff wall and pointed up.

Enthralled, he whispered, "There they are-the masks and shields and kachina gods-waiting for us."

Before us lay a group of brilliant murals from an early Indian culture, large vivid figures dressed in detailed finery, sternly staring down at us. They were indeed the gods in every way. "Brian, they are looking us over to see if we are real and as vital as they are."

He shot back, "Well, if you want to know, we are not, absolutely not. We are no way as spectacular and we do not have any illustrious future like they do. No, sir."

"The gods always win out," I remarked. "But seriously, I am serious now. I never realized how great this period of rock art could be. Its colors are vibrant, size impressive, and a vivid line encompasses those mysterious figures. I am impressed. Thank you for giving me an eye-opening experience."

"Good," he echoed, "yes, very good." Before he returned to the jeep to drive us to a picnic spot, he surveyed the area for snakes. Shifting gears over a sandy area he added, "That's why I showed them to you-so you'd like them."

"Green with envy describes me. You and your parents are lucky to be in a magical land with all this wonder to explore. Just the rock art alone is enough. How happy can one be?" I bantered, exhilarated by the pictographs.

"Except for my parents' poor health," and he grew quite complacent, "we can't complain. We have to take what we get."

I watched him become familiar, no longer on edge with me. An aberrational whim welled in me. I was taken by an irreverent urge of sheer, perverse nonsense.

"Brian," I practically mewed, "you mentioned your parents. And always with respect. Well, I should tell you something important. Did you know that your mother telephoned and told me that you held back seven santos, which you kept for yourself. And yet you forced me to pay the total amount for thirty santos. Think about that. You cheated me."

"What!" he shrieked and abruptly applied the brakes on his jeep. "What!" he bellowed, as he swerved to the left to avoid a rock. "What did you say?" he screamed, as he skidded into a tree, stopping the car. "Seven? Did you say seven?"

"Yes, seven," I replied. I felt like an idiot.

"I can't believe it. My mother actually told you about the seven santos, my good mother?" he pondered.

I solemnly nodded my head.

"My mother," he intoned in wonder. "It's hard to believe. Almost impossible."

I became extremely uncomfortable and wished I could have dived directly into the grave, or better, vanished to nothing. With my stupid mouth I lied big; I wrongly abused his dear old, faithful mother. I froze.

"If that is what she said, then it's true, every bit of it," he confessed. "My mother always tells the truth. I did remove seven santos from the group. My mother does not lie."

I quickly calmed down. Even if I was a skunk, so was he. As the result of my frivolous behavior, the real truth had emerged. He had kept extra santos and I luckily had guessed the exact number.

"Brian," I humbly apologized, "I am bad. Your mother did not talk to me about the santos. I did not speak to her at all. I devised the whole story. It is pure fiction."

"How could you?" he thundered. "You used my mother's name in vain. You crucified the very truth. You are a liar!"

"But you did keep the seven santos?" I briefly countered.

"Never mind that. Don't change the subject. Never–I don't want you ever to use her name like it is dirt, never again! Don't you dare blaspheme my mother like you did! Don't you ever!" he blistered angrily.

"I promise I won't," I conceded, "but what do you intend to do about the santos you stole from me, now that I know?"

He calmed down. "That's a different matter. We can work that out."

"I guess I can just plain buy them from you."

"Since you know now, I suppose I can sell them," he reasoned.

"I thought so–your greedy motive is pretty obvious. Alright, I will give you five thousand and no more," my voice hardened, "and you will have to take a personal check."

"Fine with me," he rejoined, and his yellow-green eyes narrowed.

While Abel and I packed the santos into the plane, Brian retrieved the missing seven. We faced each other. The propeller began to turn and whir for takeoff.

"You got what you wanted and I guess I got what I wanted," he justified the chain of events. "Although I am a little richer, I suppose we are even." He seemed contented.

"No, not at all," I chortled, "I'm way ahead. I got what I had to have, which is to me what's vital in the world. It's called art. But you are stuck with the perfunctory, the mundane, only drab scraps of green paper which anybody can obtain, since millions are printed everywhere and they all look alike. Who cares about collecting them? That's not the point."

He became uneasy again.

"Good-bye, Brian," I flipped. "Many thanks for producing no snakes and especially for showing me those remarkable pictographs." I turned and climbed into the cockpit.

He followed me. "Listen, everything fell into place. Your accountant, Jonas, told me he had talked to you about my santo collection and that you would pay me a visit, which you did. It all worked out beautifully. Since you saw the pictographs, maybe you can help me spread the word about them like they deserve. Out of all this, that's what's important." He stepped back.

As the plane taxied down the runway, I sat dazed. "Abel, he knew all along that I was going to buy his collection. I've been had-he aced me."

Then I laughed. "But you know, it simply doesn't matter after all. When I look at the santos, I think I really did better than he did, but I guess when he looks at all the money he got, he thinks he really beat me. When both sides think they have won, that's what a good trade is all about."

I stopped for a second. "And then there are the great Basketmaker pictographs. They are what art is really all about."